"Keep your head down!" Luke shouted

The helicopter was flying low behind them. The car swerved. There was another gunshot. Luke took a sharp right, and Sydney fell against the door, feeling the jolt the instant they left the pavement and hit the rocky ground, screeching to a halt. The helicopter stayed close overhead, the thunderous whirring vibrating in her ears.

Like lightning Luke was under a tree, perfectly still, his feet shoulder-length apart, his gun aimed toward a patch of blue sky between the trees. A second later he fired. Another shot. She saw the helicopter drop a few feet, then sway. Blades sputtered, and the helicopter lurched forward.

Shivering, she slowly raised her head. She couldn't see Luke at first, and alarm rose in her throat. Panic slithered down her spine. She'd heard two shots. Had Luke been shot?

The sudden thought rocked her to her core.

Dear Harlequin Intrigue Reader,

It's the most wonderful time of the year! And we have six breathtaking books this month that will make the season even brighter....

THE LANDRY BROTHERS are back! We can't think of a better way to kick off our December lineup than with this long-anticipated new installment in Kelsey Roberts's popular series about seven rascally brothers, born and bred in Montana. In *Bedside Manner*, chaos rips through the town of Jasper when Dr. Chance Landry finds himself framed for murder...and targeted for love! Check back this April for the next title, *Chasing Secrets*. Also this month, watch for *Protector S.O.S.* by Susan Kearney. This HEROES INC. story spotlights an elite operative and his ex-lover who maneuver stormy waters—and a smoldering attraction—as they race to neutralize a dangerous hostage situation.

The adrenaline keeps on pumping with *Agent-in-Charge* by Leigh Riker, a fast-paced mystery. You'll be bewitched by this month's ECLIPSE selection—*Eden's Shadow* by veteran author Jenna Ryan. This tantalizing gothic unravels a shadowy mystery and casts a magical spell over an enamored duo. And the excitement doesn't stop there! Jessica Andersen returns to the lineup with her riveting new medical thriller, *Body Search,* about two hot-blooded doctors who are stranded together in a windswept coastal town and work around the clock to combat a deadly outbreak.

Finally this month, watch for *Secret Defender* by Debbi Rawlins— a provocative woman-in-jeopardy tale featuring an iron-willed hero who will stop at nothing to protect a headstrong heiress...even kidnap her for her own good.

Best wishes for a joyous holiday season from all of us at Harlequin Intrigue.

Sincerely,

Denise O'Sullivan
Senior Editor, Harlequin Intrigue

SECRET DEFENDER
DEBBI RAWLINS

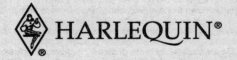

TORONTO • NEW YORK • LONDON
AMSTERDAM • PARIS • SYDNEY • HAMBURG
STOCKHOLM • ATHENS • TOKYO • MILAN • MADRID
PRAGUE • WARSAW • BUDAPEST • AUCKLAND

ISBN 0-373-22818-X

SECRET DEFENDER

Copyright © 2004 by Debbi Quattrone

www.eHarlequin.com

Printed in U.S.A.

ABOUT THE AUTHOR

Debbi Rawlins lives with her new husband in a Las Vegas suburb. She still misses Hawaii at times, mainly because of the ocean, but has come to enjoy desert living. Especially during the fall and winter months. Come summer, she heads for their Utah condo sitting 97,000 feet above the heat.

Books by Debbi Rawlins

CAST OF CHARACTERS

Sydney Wainwright—Heiress to millions. Someone is sending her threatening letters. Will she make it to her twenty-fifth birthday and claim her inheritance?

Luke Boudreau—Ex-cop, ex-con, he's kidnapped Sydney but claims he wants to protect her.

Willard Seymour—Sydney's godfather and lawyer, trusted friend of the Wainwright family who's controlled the company since the death of her parents.

Rick Wainwright—The brother Sydney didn't know she had until a year ago.

Jeff—The new man in Sydney's life—an attorney she met at a party.

Julie—An old friend from the wrong side of the tracks, who's suddenly popped into Sydney's life again.

Mama Sadie—The only person who truly knows and trusts Luke Boudreau.

This is for Karl. See? I told you I'd make
an honest man out of you.

Chapter One

Sign the papers and die.

Sydney Wainwright stared at the bold black letters on the sheet of white paper. Her hands no longer trembled like they had when she'd received the first two threats. She'd been fearful then; now, she was angry.

She wadded up the note and then slipped it in the top drawer of her desk, way in the back where no one would see it. Better that Willard and her brother didn't know she'd received another one. They'd already accused her of not taking the threats seriously enough.

They thought she should disappear for a while, go to France or Rio, or take a cruise. No way was she running scared. She'd finally taken control of her life. She wouldn't give it up that easily.

After locking the desk, she grabbed her purse and headed down the hall. She had half an hour to make it to her hair appointment. That gave Willard only two minutes to complain about her venturing out alone.

He was such a dear man, a trusted and loyal friend of the family forever, but he'd become too protective since her parents' death. He kept forgetting she wasn't a child anymore.

She stopped outside his office and knocked briefly before opening the door. Rick was sitting across from Willard's desk. They abruptly stopped talking when they saw her. Then her brother slid Willard a cryptic glance, which made her uneasy.

"Hey, what are you two doing? Conspiring against me?" She grinned, and Rick looked away.

"On your way to lunch?" Willard eyed the Chanel bag slung over her shoulder.

Rick immediately stood. "I was just on my way out, too. Let's go together."

She gave him a bland look. "Subtle, Rick." She aimed her gaze to include Willard. "I'm going to quit telling you guys when I leave the building if you keep acting this way."

"What?" Rick had the affronted-big-brother look down pat already. "I'm not supposed to break for lunch?"

She held back, instead of blasting him like she wanted to. She liked Rick, but she'd only known him for a year. It wasn't as if he'd been the big brother she'd run to all her life, but she didn't want to hurt his feelings either. His lips curved in a wry smile. He'd learned to read her quickly. "Go ahead, tell me to butt out. I can take it."

"Okay." Sydney smiled back. "Butt out."

He shook his head. "Look, I know it's hard to take, me showing up suddenly, claiming I'm your half brother. I also know Willard had me checked out down to the kind of boxers I wear before he welcomed me into the fold."

Willard didn't even blink. The attorney in him worried about her inheritance, the father in him worried about her, period. He made no apology.

Sydney chuckled. "Boring white…maybe a pair of paisley once in a while. Am I right?"

Rick didn't smile. "You can't keep treating these threats lightly, Syd. It's kind of nice having a sister, and I'd like to see you make it to your twenty-fifth birthday. Let Willard arrange for some protection until Wainwright Corporation is legally turned over to you."

Sighing, she wandered over to the window, laid her forehead against the glass and stared idly out at the Dallas skyline. Turning twenty-five should mean all a girl had to worry about was if her next date might be Mr. Right. Or whether it was time to switch to Oil of Olay.

Not worrying about gaining control of a multimillion-dollar company or division buyouts or union organizers getting ticked off because they might lose their foothold. Sydney understood the pitfalls of having that much responsibility and power, but no way did she believe the union would resort to murder. It didn't make sense.

She turned back to the earnestness in Rick's eyes. Hard to believe he was her brother. Physically, they were opposites. His eyes were blue, his hair dark blond, while she was boring brown all the way.

She pushed away from the window. "I'm not going to live in fear. I had to do that half my life. I won't do it anymore."

"This is different."

"You don't understand." Their gazes met and hers quickly skittered away.

As her father's bastard child, Rick had grown up poor while she'd been privileged with the Wainwright name and wealth. At times, guilt gnawed at her. She wasn't to blame for her father's shortcomings, of course, and Rick never showed resentment toward her. But the sad reality pricked her sense of fairness.

Rick snorted. "You're right. I don't understand living in fear of being kidnapped because I had a rich daddy who'd pay my ransom, but dammit, these threats are real. This isn't about speculation or a mere precaution. Take it seriously. Err on the side of caution, for Willard's and my sake, if not for your own."

Emotion suddenly threatened. There was no bitterness in her brother's tone. He was truly worried. After the first threat, he'd slipped into protective mode, always asking her where she was going and what time he should expect her back.

Still, it wasn't as if she was being foolish about her safety. She'd taken a self-defense course, and she never went out alone at night. Nothing was likely to happen in broad daylight. Anyway, she refused to hand over her whole life to whoever was behind these threats.

Willard had been eerily quiet and Sydney finally chanced a look at him. He stared at her over steepled fingers. Lines of tension etched his face. She was partly responsible for putting them there. Her decision to split up the company was causing some havoc, but in the long run, she knew everyone would be better off.

He'd changed since her parents' death. He worked harder, was at the office all the time. He'd assumed full responsibility for both the business and Sydney, even though she constantly assured him she did just fine on her own. Willard needed the break. He'd enjoy retirement. He already had plenty of money, and once Sydney was through, he'd have more than he could spend in three lifetimes.

"I'll think about it." She adjusted the purse strap on her shoulder. "But right now, I have to run or I'll be late."

"Where are you going?"

"None of your business. And I mean that in the nicest way."

Rick shook his head and slowly got to his feet. He looked tired. He'd been working nonstop trying to learn about the company, and now he was worrying about her.

Impulsively she gave him a peck on the cheek. "I really will think about taking a short vacation."

His mouth curved in a cynical smile. "Want me to drive you to wherever you're going?"

"No, thanks."

Rick grunted and looked at Willard. "I'll get you a sandwich."

Willard nodded, but said nothing until Rick left. "Where are you going, Sydney?"

She sighed at his impatient tone. "I have a hair appointment at Divas."

He didn't look pleased. "Don't forget we have a board meeting tonight," he said, while adjusting the cuffs of his custom-made Egyptian cotton shirt.

"Tonight?" Sydney frowned. "I thought it was tomorrow night."

"It's on your calendar."

"Yeah, but I thought it was…" She shook her head. "I'll be here."

"If you have something else planned, I could—"

"No, I was only going to have dinner with Jeff, but we can change it to tomorrow night."

At the mention of the attorney's name, Willard's gray brows came down. "You're still seeing him?"

"Still? We've only had four dates."

"I don't like him. He's a social climber. Probably more interested in your trust fund than you."

"Thanks."

"Get that phony wounded look off your face. You know the pitfalls of being in your position. I'm only looking out for your interest, and I tell you, I don't trust the man."

"You don't trust anyone." The flippant tone she used belied the heaviness in her chest. Willard was wrong. The wounded look wasn't phony at all. She knew he could be right. It wouldn't be the first time a man was more interested in her bottom line than her own bottom.

"Good thing, young lady. You're too naive."

Sydney made a face. "I'm going to forgive you for being so grumpy and overbearing because I know you have my best interest at heart. But like it or not, I'm an adult and I can make my own decisions." She blew him a kiss. "I've got to run, but I'll be back in plenty of time for the meeting."

"How are you getting there?"

She gave him a tolerant smile and left his office before he bombarded her with more questions she had no intention of answering. Besides, he'd have a cow if he found out she'd been taking cabs around town.

It was just so freeing to finally be able to make her own decisions about where she went and how she got there. It didn't mean she didn't appreciate his and Rick's concern. In fact, it had always been Willard and her mother who'd been there for her as a child. Her father had cared for her, in his own self-absorbed way, but it was her mother, Inga, who'd made sure Sydney had all the love and emotional support a child needed to grow up without prejudice or fear and with a keen sense of fairness.

It was the latter that ironically appeared to be getting Sydney into trouble. In her opinion, Wainwright Corporation had become too large, after having gobbled up smaller companies. When one of the senior vice presidents had approached her to allow him and two other executives to buy out their divisions, Sydney agreed and put the same offer on the table to all other division heads.

That's when the shit hit the fan. Willard told her she was insane. Her brother suggested she not be so impulsive. The union leaders threatened blood would be shed if they were ousted from the Wainwright factories. It all had gotten so complicated, when all she wanted to do was get a tan and count on a date every Saturday night.

The elevator dinged the moment she pressed the button and when the doors slid open, Jeff walked out with a florist's box of long-stemmed pink roses cradled in his left arm.

He smiled when he saw her. "I was coming by to see you." He eyed her purse. "On your way out?"

She nodded, her gaze falling to the roses. "I have an appointment."

"Have time to put these in water?" He leaned in for a kiss.

She gave him her cheek and then ducked his look of disappointment. She wasn't comfortable with public displays of affection…and certainly not at the office. "May I assume they're for me?"

He lowered a lazy gaze to the roses. "Possibly."

She gave him a jab to the ribs that made him grunt. "Sorry, I didn't hear you."

Jeff laughed and passed her the box.

She smiled, genuinely touched that he had come across town to hand deliver them. "Actually, I'm late, but Margaret will take care of getting them in water. Hey, take a ride with me uptown. We can talk along the way."

He held up the briefcase in his right hand. "Sorry, but I've got an appointment on the tenth floor in fifteen minutes."

"Oh." So he hadn't made a special trip. It didn't make the gesture any less sweet.

The elevator doors opened again and Jeff reclaimed the flowers. "Go. I'll give these to Margaret."

She slipped into the car before the doors closed again. "Oh, about dinner tonight. I have a board meeting. Can we make it tomorrow night?"

He shrugged. "Sure. I'll call."

The doors closed, but not before she saw annoyance enter his eyes. That barely fazed her. However, she wasn't that disappointed about tonight. Which did bother her.

Jeff was nice looking with a good sense of humor.

He was smart, a good dresser, had a terrific job with a prestigious law firm. But deep down, she knew he wasn't The One.

And dammit. She wasn't getting any younger.

SYDNEY DASHED INTO the chic salon to find Julie looking at the clock. There was no missing the woman. Her hair was shockingly red and her purple spandex dress so tight it left nothing to the imagination. She had the figure to pull it off, though. When Sydney had first met her in prep school, Julie's hair had been brown and she'd been a little chubby. Now, she looked as if she'd stepped off the pages of *Cosmo*.

Julie put her hands on her hips as soon as she saw Syd. "You're late."

"Only four minutes." Sydney moved her hand from behind her back. "And only because I stopped to get you this."

Julie's black-rimmed green eyes lit up at the sight of the iced mocha latte and she quickly snatched it out of Syd's hand. "Okay, I forgive you."

"Gee, thanks." Sydney stashed her purse on a shelf next to Julie's blow-dryer and then took a seat in front of the mirror. She stared at her drab hair color and noticed her complexion was pretty dull, too. She needed to apply more of that self-tanning stuff.

"I hope you've cleared at least two hours this afternoon." Julie shook out a black cape and draped it over Syd, and then frowned. "Maybe you ought to wear a smock today."

"Two hours? For a trim?"

"I decided to put in some highlights." Julie picked up

a lock of Syd's hair and inspected it with pursed lips. "I think a nice light ash blond will work."

"You decided?" She laughed, and jerked her head away. "I'm not ready for highlights. Besides, I don't have the time."

"Bull." Julie brought out a tube of hair color and squirted it into a silver bowl. "Hey, when are you going to introduce me to that brother of yours?"

Syd sighed. "I honestly don't have time."

Julie stopped mixing to give her a sour look. "So, what—you think I'm not good enough for the heir apparent?"

"I didn't deserve that remark." Syd stiffened. "Anyway, I meant I don't have time for the highlights."

The other woman blinked and, muttering a curse, ducked her head. "You're right. I shouldn't have said that."

"But that's what you think." She tried to keep the hurt from her voice, but she failed. Miserably, by the look of alarm on Julie's face.

"I don't. Honest." Julie shook her head and put down the bowl. "Not you, of all people. You took me under your wing when none of the other girls would give me the time of day." She ignored Sydney's dismissive wave. "I've never forgotten that, Syd. I swear to God. I'm having a shitty day and I took it out on you."

"That's okay. No problem." Sydney shrugged it off. It really wasn't a big deal.

Shaking her head, Julie busied herself with mixing and stirring the color. She was still angry with herself, Sydney could tell by the jerky motions she used. Self-reproach was a habit Julie had established early.

Sydney vividly remembered the day they'd met. Julie

had been outgoing, full of joie de vivre. They'd both turned fifteen that summer, and Julie had just moved to Plano after her mother had married a prominent attorney she'd met at a restaurant where she waited tables. Life had changed instantly for them.

They'd traded their beat-up, ten-year-old VW for a bronze Mercedes and moved from a one-bedroom apartment downtown to a twenty-room mansion. Next, Julie's stepfather enrolled her in the same prep school as Sydney, whose snotty classmates had been less than kind.

Julie looked up suddenly, her smile returning. "You're good people, Syd, even if you are filthy rich."

"Gee, thanks."

Julie laughed. "Remember Samantha Bellamy?"

"Please." Sydney sighed. "Don't even bring her up."

"Friggin' snob. Treated me as though I had some kind of contagious disease. Wouldn't invite you to her birthday party if you took me, and you told her to go to hell." She grunted. "Your daddy had more money than all the rest of those goddamn snobs put together."

"Can we change the subject?"

Julie thoughtfully studied the color she'd mixed. "I'd like to get her in my chair for a couple of hours. Maybe I could send her an offer for a free color."

Sydney laughed. "Don't even think about it."

At least Julie had developed a sense of humor over the whole mess. True, it had been years ago, but the girls had been exceptionally cruel. Sydney simply had been embarrassed. She'd thought she knew those girls, considered several of them among her friends…until she saw how ugly they could be.

She and Julie had become fast friends from that moment on and did everything together. At the close of their senior year everything changed.

Julie's fairy-tale life ended with her mom and stepfather's divorce, and she landed back "across the tracks." Not only that, but Julie had changed. She seemed bitter and hateful, claiming it was her fault but never explaining why.

Sydney had her own theories about the stepfather's inordinate affection for Julie, but Julie refused to talk about it. In fact, she eventually failed to return Sydney's phone calls and headed to California.

Julie set the bowl of color aside and put her hands on her hips. "When I get through with you, you are going to look so hot, girlfriend."

Sydney frowned. "What if I don't like it? Will you be able to dye it back to my natural color?"

"Back to this mousy brown? Why the hell would you want to do that?"

"I wish you wouldn't be so coy about your feelings."

Julie laughed. "You have nondescript brown hair. That's not exactly front-page news."

"I'm serious, Jules. What if I hate it?"

"You won't." Julie pinched several strands of Sydney's hair and inspected them.

Oh, God, she had a board meeting to attend. She didn't want to go looking like some… She jerked when Julie picked up a small paintbrush and put it near Sydney's hair. "I didn't say okay yet."

"Don't be a chickenshit. This is for your own good."

"Toni did my hair for years and never suggested highlights."

"Toni was afraid to say boo to you."

Sydney frowned. "Why?"

Julie chuckled. "You're cute, smart, rich, but talk about naive." With a hand on her shoulder, Julie forced her to sit back. "Who around here is gonna tell a Wainwright what to do?"

"You."

"Exactly. Now shut up while I do what I do best."

Sydney bristled as she considered what Julie said. "People aren't afraid to talk to me."

Julie rolled her gaze toward the ceiling. "If you say so."

"They aren't." Sydney settled back, stewing. She tried her darnedest to be like everyone else. Willard criticized her for it, reminding her she was a Wainwright. But Julie wouldn't lie. That was the thing Sydney liked best. Julie was a straight-talker.

It was like a miracle when she'd shown up several months ago at the salon Sydney had used for years. They'd both been surprised, but after a few awkward moments, their friendship resumed.

Meeting Julie at fifteen had been a turning point in Sydney's life. The personal exposure to someone outside her social class had taught Syd more than her four years at Yale. It had taught her that money didn't just mean power and privilege, but an enormous responsibility toward others.

"Okay, just a few highlights. In the back."

Julie grinned and separated a strip of Sydney's bangs. Sydney sighed.

"Who's the professional here? Just sit back and tell me about that hunky brother of yours."

Sydney couldn't help but smile. After blossoming at

sixteen, Julie had always gotten any guy she wanted, and she did it with such relish. "Tell you what. Come over for dinner Saturday night and see for yourself."

Julie lifted a brow but kept working, inserting the piece of foil under the strands she separated. "So he's living at the house. I take it he finally has old Willy's stamp of approval."

"You can't blame Willard for checking him out. It was a little odd that Rick showed up after my dad's death, claiming to be his illegitimate son."

Julie wrinkled her nose. "It was kind of creepy."

"Not creepy, just strange. Kind of convenient, with Dad not here to deny the claim, you know?" Sydney shrugged, her gaze glued to Julie's busy hands. "But somehow I knew Rick would check out. I'm glad, too."

"You always did have great instincts about people. What about this Jeff guy you've been seeing? When do I meet him?"

Sydney groaned. "You're starting to sound like Willard. I'll make sure they're both there on Saturday."

"Will Willy be there, too?"

"Why?"

"He doesn't like me."

"That's not true."

"Sit still before you make me spill this stuff." Julie gave her hair a small yank. "He really doesn't like me. Never has, and after I started working here, he had me checked out, too."

Sydney gasped. "I don't believe that."

"Sit still, dammit."

"Ouch! Quit yanking so hard."

"Then stop moving."

Sydney twisted around in the chair to look Julie in the eyes. "Why do you think he had you checked out?"

A sly smile curved her ruby-tinted lips. "Because I screwed the detective he hired."

Sydney blinked. "You're making this up."

Julie put her hands on either side of Sydney's head and forced her to face the mirror again. "I am not. Ask Willard. But, God, don't tell him I slept with the guy or he'll hire someone else and I'll have to go through it all over again."

Sydney stared at her reflection in simmering silence. Willard had always been overprotective, but spying on her friends pushed the limit of Sydney's patience. She ought to pack up and move to New York. Out of his sight. Away from the Wainwright name.

"I shouldn't have told you." Julie stopped fussing with the foil squares and gave her a thoughtful frown. "Don't blame Willard. It really is a pretty big coincidence that I'd show up in a salon you used after all these years. Don't you think?"

Syd quickly averted her gaze.

Julie snorted. "It's okay. I'd be suspicious, too."

"I'm not suspicious." She wasn't. "But I did wonder if you knew I'd been coming here…"

Julie shook her head. "Nope. I knew Divas had an up-scale clientele with prices to match, which meant I could make some serious dough." She set aside the bowl and brush. "One thing I did learn from old McKenzie was how to appreciate the finer things in life. Paying for them is something else."

Sydney was startled to hear her mention her former stepfather. Even before the divorce, speaking his name was taboo. Julie's hatred for him had exploded so quickly that Syd had wondered if something more had been going on than Julie had revealed.

"Hey, want me to add some purple tint?" Julie asked, and Syd made a move to get out of the chair. "Only kidding. Sit still and I'll have you out of here in under two hours."

Sydney smiled, glad Julie had come back into her life. She needed someone quirky to offset the staidness that accompanied the Wainwright name. Someone comfortable enough to point out Syd had mousy brown hair.

They chatted nonstop for the next two hours, Syd begging unsuccessfully to face the mirror while Julie blew her hair dry.

Sydney was actually starting to get a little nervous when Julie finally said, "Voila, check out this masterpiece."

She twirled the chair so that Sydney faced her reflection. Her hand automatically flew to her hair. "You cut it different."

"Did I?" Julie grinned. "Faboo, isn't it?"

Sydney stared at the unfamiliar image. Golden highlights framed her face, making her complexion look brighter. The style was artfully tousled, kind of fringed and shaggy on the side instead of her usual blunt bob. "Wow! Is that me?"

"You like?"

"I think so."

Julie issued a sound of disgust. "It's terrific. You'll turn every head from here to your office."

Right. Sydney turned from side to side, and then used the hand mirror Julie gave her. "I do look pretty sophisticated." She leaned toward the mirror for a closer look. "You did good."

"Yes, I did." Julie pulled the cape off Syd. "Now, get out of my chair. I have another client and your ride is waiting."

"My ride?" She slid off the chair and grabbed her purse.

"I had the receptionist call you a car so you wouldn't have to take a cab."

"And if I wanted to take a cab?"

"Tough. That's one of those fou-fou things they do around here that makes a friggin' haircut cost three times what it should."

Sydney laughed and pressed some bills into Julie's hand. Thankfully, she didn't argue about the tip like she had the past two times. "See you for dinner on Saturday, huh?" Sydney said as she took one last look at her reflection.

"Sure." Julie's half shrug was noncommittal.

"I'll make sure Willard isn't there."

"You look terrific. Now, get out of here."

Julie's next client approached, and Sydney stepped aside. She wanted to encourage Julie to come to dinner but it would be too awkward. Instead, she left to pay her bill.

A black Lincoln Town Car with tinted windows was waiting just outside the door and she quickly got in without getting her hair too mussed up. "I'm going to the Wainwright building on—"

"I know where it is." The driver's voice was deep and raspy and sent an odd shiver down Sydney's spine.

She sank back against the seat and stared at the back of his dark head. He barely cleared the top of the car, which meant he had to be pretty tall. The usual white cotton shirt most drivers wore stretched across his broad shoulders. His hair was long, a little too long, enough to make a ponytail, she guessed. Not that it mattered but...

"Excuse me." She snapped out of her daydreaming and squinted out the window. They were on the freeway. "You're going the wrong way."

"No, we're not," he said in that deep husky voice.

And then she heard the definitive click of all four locks engaging.

Chapter Two

Fear tightened Sydney's chest. Bile rose in her throat. She stared at his large tanned hand gripping the wheel. "You're going the wrong way," she said again, her voice sounding pathetically, maddeningly weak.

"Relax. I'm not going to hurt you." His eyes met hers in the rearview mirror. They were icy blue. "As long as you cooperate."

"What do you want?"

"Just your cooperation."

"I have money...cash in my purse, and credit cards." She fumbled with the stubborn catch on her pocketbook. "You can have them all." Her frantic gaze flew to the window. They were already passing the city limits. "Just leave me here on the side of the road."

His laugh was humorless, dark. "Sweetheart, some things money can't buy."

Nausea rolled in her stomach, but she tried to stay focused. There was a narrow space between the pair of tinted glass dividers separating them. If she could wedge her hand between them...

Her purse clasp finally gave, startling her. A tube of

lipstick and a roll of breath mints spilled out. She reached in for her wallet, hoping she could still tempt him with cash. That's when she felt it.

The barrel of the small gun Rick had bought her.

She'd argued with him at the time. She'd always been opposed to carrying a weapon of any kind, but she'd finally given in to placate him.

The pistol was in a separate pocket and she slowly disengaged the zipper. With her other hand, she fisted a wad of bills, and then held the cash up for his view.

"Look," she said, hoping he'd reconsider. If not, it was still a good distraction. "There's about five hundred dollars here."

His eyes again met hers in the mirror. The corners crinkled. "I already have you *and* the money."

She finally worked the gun free, dropped the money and pointed the pistol with both shaky hands at his head. "But I have this."

A brief look of surprise entered his eyes. He said nothing but swerved the car off the freeway onto the shoulder. He didn't stop, but drove through the tall grass toward a dense patch of trees and shrubs.

Two cars flew by them down the freeway. They didn't look as though they planned to stop. Fear clogged her throat and she had to swallow hard in order to speak. "Stop right now or I swear I'll shoot."

He drove another ten yards and parked the car in the middle of a grove of oak trees, which effectively concealed them from other motorists.

He threw open his door and got out, and then opened hers. Without a word, he reached in and grabbed one of her wrists and dragged her out. Startled, she almost dropped the gun.

But she managed to hold on to it and as soon as her feet were planted in the grass, she aimed the barrel at him. "I mean it."

"Or what?" One side of his mouth lifted in a cocky grin. His chin and jaw were dark with stubble, his long hair unruly, his amused blue eyes boring into her. He didn't seem the least bit concerned.

"Or I'll shoot that smug smile off your face." Hell, she should have said *goddamn smile*. Julie would have. It sounded more forceful.

He didn't so much as flinch. He just stared at her, until his gaze dropped to her chest. It stayed there a long time before he lazily let it roam her waist, her hips...the juncture of her thighs.

"I mean it." She swallowed. "You dumb son of a bitch."

His gaze shot up to her face, and before she knew what happened, he yanked the gun out of her hand.

"If you wanna shoot someone, sweetheart, you'd better release the safety first." He inspected the pistol. "Bullets would help, too."

He reached behind and stuck the gun in the back pocket of his jeans. From his other pocket, he produced a pair of handcuffs.

"Oh, no." She took a step back. "Please don't."

He didn't even bother to stop her. He had on cowboy boots. She had on heels. He knew she wouldn't get far.

"It was your choice." He slowly unfastened the cuffs, as if he were deliberately trying to torture her.

Even though she knew it was useless, she took another step back. "Just tell me what you want. We can work something out."

He smiled and advanced. "Come on, Sydney, a bright girl like you can figure it out."

He'd used her name.

She stood frozen, numb with fear, the slim hope that this was a random mugging shriveling inside her. Her knees weakened and her legs started to wobble.

The man stopped directly in front of her, inches away, his breath scented with the sweet surreal smell of butterscotch. Something odd flickered in his eyes, and he wrapped his arms around her. She started to struggle, but he held her to his chest. Belying his cool exterior, his heart pounded against her ear.

"Settle down. I'm just trying to keep you from ending up in a heap," he said, and loosened his hold when she pulled back.

She lifted her chin and willed her legs to stop shaking. "I'm fine."

"Good." He reached around her and caught her wrists.

Her breasts crushed against his hard chest. "Oh, please don't cuff them behind my back. You know I can't get away."

He stared down at her, his gaze wary and measuring. He was taller than she first thought...at least six-two because she was five-five and he towered over her.

"Okay." He released her wrists and stepped back.

"Thank you." Her voice had come out barely above a whisper. She pushed her hair back and was about to smooth her skirt when he grabbed her hands again. "What are you doing?"

He slapped the cuffs around one wrist and then the other. "I'm not going to leave you free to bushwhack me."

"But I—"

He put the rough pad of his thumb against her lips. "One more word and I cuff those pretty little hands of yours behind your back."

She swallowed and remained silent.

His gaze stayed on her face as he dragged his thumb across the seam of her lips before lowering it. "Get back in the car."

She hesitated, wanting to ask where they were going and who he represented, but the warning gleam in his eyes stopped her cold. Instead, she went back to the car and climbed into the backseat. When her skirt rode up high on her thigh, his blatant gaze followed the hem until she tugged it down.

A mocking smile curved his mouth. "Don't worry, Sydney, your virtue isn't what I'm after."

"What is it? What do you want?"

"For you to keep your mouth shut." He grabbed her purse, then slammed the door and got back behind the wheel.

Sydney's angry glare seared the back of his head. It didn't seem to bother him in the slightest. He steered them back toward the highway, eyed her in the mirror while he waited for a group of cars to pass, and then eased in behind a truck.

She thought about trying to flag someone down, but the windows were heavily tinted and she figured she'd just end up ticking him off. She could only hope he wasn't stupid enough to harm her. If a ransom was what he was after, he'd have to keep her alive. At least for a while.

She shuddered at the thought of what could happen once he got the money. Oh, God, she didn't want to die. She wanted to get married, have children, her own home. She wanted to go to a PTA meeting. Hell, she couldn't die without ever having had great sex.

Forcing herself to calm down, she took several deep breaths. She had to clear her head. Negative thinking wasn't going to help her find a means of escape.

From the self-defense course she'd taken, she recalled the instructor advising the class to humanize the situation. Force the attacker to view you as a human being and not an object. It was worth a shot.

She cleared her throat. "What's your name?"

His eyes appeared in the rear view mirror. "Why?"

"I've got to call you something."

"I'm sure you've come up with several names by now."

"At least."

Again, the skin around his eyes crinkled. So, he had a sense of humor. "Luke."

"Short for Lucas?"

"No."

Sydney sank back, thinking of what else she should ask or say. She wasn't going to get anywhere fast if he kept giving her single word answers. "Can you tell me who you work for?"

"No."

"I didn't think so," she muttered. "How about where we're going?"

"You'll see soon enough."

Personal. She needed to get personal so he'd see her as a person. "How old are you?"

In the rearview mirror, she saw his dark brows draw together. "Why?"

She shrugged. "I was just curious. I'll be twenty-five next month. It's kind of a milestone, don't you think?"

He shook his head and stared at the road.

Let him think she was a nut. At least he'd be thinking of her as a person. "My godfather is planning this big party he doesn't think I know about. I hate those things. I'm seriously thinking about escaping to San Francisco or New York for the weekend. Knowing that crowd, they won't even miss me."

He darted a glance at her and then returned his attention to the road as he veered off an exit ramp. Unfamiliar with the area, she squinted to see where they were going, but it was too late. She'd missed the name of the exit.

Dammit. She should be paying attention. If she had the opportunity to use a phone, she'd have to be able to give information. She looked out helplessly as the landscape became more and more dense with trees. Not a single car had passed since they left the freeway.

"Are you from Dallas?" she asked, annoyed that her teeth chattered. "You have a little bit of an accent."

The warning look he gave her with those steely blue eyes made her pause. Okay, maybe that was too personal. Obviously, he wouldn't give her that kind of information about himself. "How much ransom are you going to ask for?"

The car jerked when he pulled it over to the shoulder. Unprepared, she fell roughly against the door. There'd be one heck of a bruise on her arm.

He got out before she righted herself, opened the door and leaned in, bringing his face close to hers. He gripped her upper arm and yanked her even closer. "Do I have to gag you?"

She had to tilt her head back to avoid smashing her nose into his chin. His breath, warm and sweet-smelling, trespassed on her skin. She swallowed and shook her head.

His eyes bore into hers. "I didn't hear you."

She swallowed again. "No."

His grip on her arm loosened and he rubbed his thumb idly just beneath her sleeve hem. Irritation simmered in his eyes, and then he abruptly let her go. "Keep your mouth shut. Got it?"

She nodded, not trusting herself to speak.

He drew back, and then hesitated. He leaned in again and she jumped. "Look," he said, keeping a little more distance this time, his husky voice soft, soothing. "You're not going to get hurt. Just keep quiet."

She nodded again, hating the fear that clawed at her, robbing her of speech and rational thought. Never would she have guessed she'd react this way. All the times Willard had warned her of something like this happening, she'd balked, telling herself exactly how she'd handle the situation. Reality was nothing like her best intentions.

Relief eased her when he finally turned to get back behind the wheel, except he reached in for something and returned.

She tried not to cower and sat perfectly still.

"Here." He held out a bottle of Evian.

She stared at it a moment before lifting her bound hands to take it. "Thank you."

It was obvious she wouldn't be able to unscrew the cap, but she wouldn't ask him to do it. She just wanted him to get back in the front seat, away from her.

He grunted something that sounded like a curse and grabbed the water. After he freed the cap, he passed the bottle back to her. "We'll be at the cabin soon."

Cabin? She stared off into the woods, all hope of attracting someone's attention fading as quickly as the late afternoon sun.

He got back in and started to drive, his attention to the speed limit somewhat lax. Half the water she tried to drink missed her mouth and ended up down the front of her favorite peach silk blouse. No doubt it was ruined. But of course, that was the least of her worries.

She tried to pay attention to her surroundings, but it didn't help. Nothing but woods stretched in every direction. She didn't have a clue where they were. She glanced at her watch. They were already almost an hour outside of Dallas.

Twenty minutes later, he pulled off onto a dirt road with enough dips and ruts to make her stomach roll. She swallowed hard against the nausea, and then took another sip of water. When a cabin appeared in a small clearing, she didn't know if she were more relieved or nervous.

He stopped the car a few feet from the tiny front porch, got out and opened her door. "I wouldn't bother screaming. There's no one around for miles."

She hesitated, sweeping a gaze around the shabby condition of the property. Half the first step up to the porch had rotted away, and a couple of floorboards were missing near the faded orange lawn chair sitting by the door.

"Sorry the accommodations don't suit you." He held out his hand to help her out. "But you'll be comfortable enough inside."

His mocking tone made her straighten, and she scooted across the seat to get out…without his help. Except her skirt slid up her thigh, giving him quite an eyeful.

He wasn't shy about taking it, either. His gaze wrapped around her legs before she was able to tug the hem back down. When he realized that she didn't want his help, he stepped aside and folded his arms across his chest.

Muscle corded and stretched up his exposed forearms to where he'd turned back his shirtsleeves. Right below his elbow, a long scar marred his tanned skin. It was straight and precise, as if it were made by a knife, but jagged enough that no doctor would have made the incision.

At the thought, she fought back a shudder. Her circle of friends did not include anyone like him. He was a physical man. She could see that just by the way he stood there, his arms folded across his broad chest, his legs parted as he rested confidently on the heels of his tan cowboy boots. Problems were likely solved with his hands and not intellectually. She'd do well to remember that.

No designer label tagged his faded jeans, either. They were worn, soft looking, until they fitted him like a kid glove. Worn enough that she could see how the muscle bulged above his knee and traveled up his thigh. Her gaze snagged on his fly, and she quickly looked away, keeping her eyes averted as she set her feet on the ground.

She made sure her footing was solid before she stood. Only then did she look up at him. He was staring at her chest. She had modest-sized breasts at best;

nothing a man generally gave a second look at. She glanced down to see what had grabbed his attention.

The front of her blouse was soaked, the now transparent silk clinging to her pink lace bra. In the center of each breast, her nipples were dark and budding—and clearly visible.

She gasped and turned to the side. But not before she caught the annoyed look in his eyes.

"If you want to stand here all night, I could cuff you to the car door."

His voice was gruff, impatient, and she moved toward the cabin without looking at him. She hesitated when she got to the rotting first step.

Behind her, she heard the trunk open. Paper rustled, and then something thudded to the ground. She glanced over her shoulder. He was taking a bag out of the trunk. Without giving the impulse a second thought, she kicked off her heels and dashed toward a thicket of trees.

She'd made it just a few yards when he grabbed her around the waist and they both hit the ground. His body pressed hers into the hard earth. She clawed the grass, struggling to get out from under him. Dirt packed under her nails, and her knees stung where gravel scraped her skin.

"Stupid, Sydney, very stupid." He got up and yanked her upright. He pulled her so close she had to tilt her head back. "How far did you think you'd get?"

She forced her eyes to meet the fire in his and hoped he didn't smell her fear. "You didn't really expect me to roll over and play dead, did you?"

"Look." He fisted her blouse and brought her closer. "I'm not going to hurt you." He stared down at her, and she flinched when he raised his other hand. He flicked some grass off her cheek. "Unless I have to."

"That's supposed to be reassuring?"

"Just cooperate, dammit." He let her go so abruptly she stumbled backward, her cuffed hands useless to help maintain her balance. He made no move to catch her. "Get inside."

Her shoulder hit a tree trunk hard, but at least she stayed on her feet. She bit back the remark that nearly glided off her tongue. It was a snooty thought that surprised her. But he seemed just so damned earthy. Primal. He was out of her experience, and she hated feeling at such a loss.

Instead, she edged toward the porch, stooping to pick up her black Ferragamo pumps and discreetly spitting out the dirt in her mouth. The rotting steps were tricky, but she gingerly maneuvered them without ending up on her fanny. The door was slightly ajar, and she pushed it with her toe. It creaked open farther and she peeked inside before crossing the threshold.

The room was small. Nothing separated the kitchen area from the old army-green couch or the unmade double bed. There was one door that she assumed led to a bathroom. As she got farther inside, she was surprised by the cleanliness of everything from the ancient wood floor to the single kitchen countertop. No dust or grime was visible, and in fact, the portable refrigerator was smudge-free and shiny. Odd.

Sydney was a bigger mess. Mud coated her blouse and skin, thanks to the water she'd spilled. A few gobs were in her hair—her newly shampooed and styled hair. Darn it.

When she heard Luke step up on the porch, she moved quickly to give him a wide berth. She saw then that the door did lead to a bathroom. An absurdly tiny one, but at least it had a tub and a door.

"I have some things here for you."

His voice startled her, even though she knew he was inside. The place was just so damn small, and he was so big. She glanced at the bed again. Only one. A double. She hoped he wasn't…

"Are you listening?"

She slid him a glance and nodded.

He held a medium-sized black leather bag. As if reading her thoughts, his gaze went briefly to the bed, then back to her. "There are a few shirts and shorts in here and some toiletries. Let me know if you need anything else."

"How considerate."

At her sarcasm, his left brow went up. "I'll get us something to eat in about an hour."

"You leaving?"

For the first time, his mouth curved slightly, and his gaze lowered. "Don't worry. I'll be here all night."

Sydney swallowed. "There's only one bed."

He glanced at it in mock surprise. "So there is."

"Where will you sleep?"

"Right next to you, darlin'." His smile broadened as he tossed the bag on the bed. "We're having sandwiches tonight." He eyed her with misgiving. "Unless you know how to cook."

She gritted her teeth. "I have to go to the bathroom."

"You saw it."

"Can you unlock the handcuffs?"

"Nope."

"But we're stuck in the middle of God knows where." She sounded breathless, afraid. She hated that.

"If you need help, just holler."

Like hell. She turned away and unzipped the black bag. She took the first shirt on top. It was denim. Not one of his, but brand new, a size small—something he might have bought for her. Next, she pulled out a hairbrush and toothbrush, and wondered if all kidnappers went through this much trouble.

She kept the things away from her wet, muddy blouse, and without looking at him, headed inside the bathroom. The back of the toilet was the only available surface, so she draped the shirt on the doorknob and set the brushes near the sink faucet. When she tried to swing the door shut, something blocked it from closing.

Poking her head around, she saw the toe of Luke's boot pressed to the bottom of the door. Her gaze slowly traveled up the worn denim covering his leg, to the white shirt he'd partially unbuttoned, to the exposed wedge of smooth muscled chest, to the strong, square, stubbled jaw.

She finally met his eyes just as he said, "Leave it open."

Chapter Three

Sydney stared back at him. "What did you say?"

"Leave the door open."

"Why?"

"In case you get stupid again."

"I've learned my lesson." At his implacable expression, her heart pounded and her palms grew damp. He couldn't possibly expect her to leave herself that vulnerable. "There's only one small window in here—"

"Big enough for you to crawl out."

"It's too narrow."

He ran his gaze down her body, lingering around her hips, studying her every curve until her insides trembled. "The door stays open."

"I can't go to the bathroom with you out here and— I can't do it."

"We're going to be here a week. Get over it."

"A week?" She swallowed, but her mouth was so dry the act was painful. "And then what?" She tried another painful swallow. "Are you going to kill me?"

His brows came down in impatience. "I already said I wouldn't hurt you."

"Wh-what…" She stopped and took a quick breath, despising how weak she sounded. "What are you going to do with me?"

He studied her a moment. "Nothing, as long as you cooperate."

"But—"

"No more talking."

She had no choice. She had to believe he wouldn't hurt her, as foolish or naive as that seemed. Backing up, she caught her bedraggled reflection in the mirror above the sink. Mud smeared her cheek. She looked at him again. He had smudges on his shirt and dirt in his hair. "Can't you just bolt the window from the outside?"

He laughed. It was more a grunt. "Don't worry. I'm not interested in any of your goods."

He walked away as if the matter were closed, and she stood watching him, horrified that his demeaning remark stung. Anger simmered with the fear churning in her stomach. At least he'd moved away from her.

"By the way." At the kitchen counter, he began unloading a paper sack. "If I so much as hear the door creak, I'll take it off the hinges."

"Why are you being so cruel?"

He looked sharply at her.

She cleared her throat, hoping to sound more assertive. "You already have me. It's unnecessary to be so…unkind."

Frowning, he shoved the sack aside. "Cruel?"

"Why do I need to be handcuffed *and* have the door open? Are you that afraid of me?"

His sudden bark of laughter startled her. "All right."

He dug into his jeans' pocket, and her gaze helplessly drew to the worn denim straining across his fly.

She blinked and raised her gaze, unsettled by the jittery feeling in her tummy.

He produced a small key and started toward her. Her first impulse was to run; instead, she stepped outside and held up her bound hands, anxious to be free of the cuffs. He scanned the front of her muddy, wet shirt before inserting the key. "Do anything foolish again, and I'll—" His gaze fastened on the inside of her wrists. "What the hell?"

He quickly unlocked the cuffs and picked up her right hand, turning it over to expose the ugly rash spreading across her skin. "These cuffs weren't that tight."

His eyes met hers and she was amazed to see concern softening his expression. He looked back down at her wrist, then picked up her other hand and inspected the reddening skin there.

"I'm allergic to some kinds of metal," she said, alarmed at how close he was, how gently he soothed the surrounding skin with the pad of his thumb.

He lifted his gaze to hers, a mixture of suspicion and confusion darkening his eyes. "You should have told me."

She shrugged, but hope bubbled inside her. He really didn't intend to hurt her. He wouldn't be concerned otherwise.

Abruptly, he dropped her hands and jerked his head toward the bathroom. "Go ahead. I'll be in the kitchen."

"You won't—" She cut herself off. It was silly to ask him not to peek.

After giving her a long, hard look, he turned away.

Sydney hurried back inside the bathroom and almost closed the door out of habit. She stopped herself, convinced he'd have no qualms about doing exactly what he said he would. Unable to resist a final glance, she saw him busy unloading the grocery sack, facing away from her.

She'd started to unbutton her blouse when she realized that she needed a bath. Mud was caked and drying in some uncomfortable places. But with the door open? Not in this lifetime.

"Luke?" Saying his name felt odd. Too intimate.

"Yeah?"

"I need to take a bath."

"Good idea."

Anger coiled in her belly. She hated having to practically ask his permission to do something so personal, and then get an editorial. "I can't do it with the door open."

His sigh was loud, impatient. "Too bad."

She could get around a bath by washing at the sink. Certainly not her preference but under the circumstances...

"And don't think about skipping the bath. I don't want you messing up the sheets the first night here."

Tempted to give him an obscene hand sign she'd never given anyone in her life, she gritted her teeth. He didn't have to know what she was doing in here. She'd use the tub, all right, by sitting on the edge...with her clothes on. She kicked aside the bath rug and leaned over to turn on the faucet. It wouldn't budge. She sat, hoping for better leverage. Still no luck.

"It's a little tricky." Luke's voice directly behind her made her jump. "Let me get it."

She started to move out of the way, but he reached

over her. His shoulder brushed her breast and she stiffened. Oblivious to the contact, he worked at trying to get the spigot to turn. Muscles corded and bunched on his arm. She could smell his heat, feel the powerful energy he radiated; to her absolute shame, she had an undeniable feminine reaction.

"Sweetheart, you're going to have to move."

She abruptly raised her gaze to his. An odd little gleam lurked there. Amusement, perhaps? She took a deep, steadying breath and nearly shoved him aside. "I was trying to do that before you crowded me." Shoving, however, would require touching. She straightened her spine. "Excuse me, please."

One side of his mouth lifted as he stepped back and motioned her around him. "That's far enough," he said, when she backed out of the door. "I'd hate to have to cuff you to the towel rack."

That made her plant her feet, and she absently rubbed her reddened wrists. She didn't want those cuffs on again. She'd cooperate all right, unless the perfect opportunity to escape presented itself. God, she hoped she wasn't wrong, but she truly believed he wouldn't harm her. This guy didn't seem to be any ordinary thug. Her intuition told her otherwise.

He finally got the faucet turned, and water trickled slowly into the tub. It was clear, as though someone had run it recently. Luke turned the spigot some more, and the water pressure increased.

"It's going to take about a minute to warm up." He straightened and moved back. She ducked out of his way. He looked over at her, his gaze roaming her body. "It should be ready by the time you undress."

It wasn't an insolent look, or even a suggestive one, but it gave her goose bumps. "Thank you."

"When you're done, I'll take my shower while the water's still hot," he said, and she must have shown some kind of reaction because the amusement was back in his eyes.

She stepped around him to go back into the bathroom and then turned to look pointedly at him.

"You don't have anything I haven't seen before," he said with a mocking smile and headed toward the kitchen area.

Sydney resisted temptation and kept her mouth shut. She scooted as far away from the door as possible and unbuttoned her blouse. Across her chest there were several small red blotches. Nerves did that to her sometimes. Sitting in cool water would help, but having to take off all her clothes with an open door would probably produce another crop of hives.

Quickly, she shrugged out of her blouse and slid off her skirt, casting several glances out the door. Luke was nowhere in sight. Even so, she left her bra and panties on. There wasn't much to the scraps of peach-colored silk and lace; wet, they'd be totally transparent. Still, it made her feel less vulnerable to keep them on.

She adjusted the spigot to keep the water from getting too warm, and when it tested perfect, she splashed water on her face and chest, letting the tepid water soothe her fevered skin.

"Are you decent?"

Luke's voice was entirely too close and she looked around for something to cover herself. "No!" Her blouse was just out of reach. She crossed her arms over her chest. "What do you want?"

"I forgot to give you a towel."

"Leave it outside the door."

"I'll toss it on the sink."

"No, just—"

His arm appeared, and panicked, she slid down into the claw foot tub. But he merely laid the navy blue towel on the corner of the sink and then withdrew. She couldn't see the rest of him, but knowing he was that close was unnerving.

"Did I leave you soap?"

God, couldn't he just go! She straightened a little to check the sink and found nothing. The soap dish for the tub had...

She screamed.

"Sydney?" Luke came through the door like a rocket. "Sydney?"

"Get out!"

He stood over her, his gaze sweeping her body. "What the hell is wrong?"

"Nothing." Her crossed arms seemed useless under his piercing blue eyes. "It's a spider, but it's dead. Go."

"What's that?" He stared at the blotches on her chest.

"Nothing. Please leave."

His eyes met hers, and she was surprised to see uncertainty etched in his face. "You need something for it?"

She blinked. This might be the opportunity she needed. "Yes...medicine. I'll get horribly sick without it."

His brows furrowed slightly, and then his expression relaxed. "Sorry, sweetheart, you're a lousy liar." He glanced at his watch. "I'll give you ten minutes. And then I come in after you."

His gaze lowered to her crossed arms again before he turned and walked out.

LUKE CUT INTO the tomato and nearly took the tip of his thumb off. He cursed loudly and threw aside the knife. Meat and cheese were all anyone needed in a damn sandwich, anyway. If it was good enough for him, it was good enough for Sydney Wainwright.

She wasn't what he'd expected. She didn't look or sound or smell rich. Maybe because she'd always been rolling in dough. Not like the Hollywood nouveau riche he was used to. The kind that had to let everyone know they had more than you. She hadn't even complained about being allergic to the cuffs. That had shocked the hell out of him.

No matter. He was being paid well for this job and that's all he cared about. After he collected the other half of his fee, he'd think about a short trip to Brazil. Settling old scores always helped him to sleep better.

He finished making the sandwiches and sealed them in plastic. Next, he got out a couple of cold colas and a beer. Sydney had been in the tub for almost fifteen minutes. He really ought to yank her out so she'd know he meant business, but he hadn't counted on her breaking out in a nervous rash.

He swore to himself. That better be all it was. His gaze wandered toward the bathroom at the same moment she stepped out of the tub. He knew because he saw her reflection in the mirror as her head came up. Taking a pull of beer, he started to turn away, but caught a glimpse of her bare breasts.

Small, but round and full, they stood out firm,

crowned by two large rosy nipples. They were damn near perfect. He swallowed and told himself to look away. It was the decent thing to do.

But he stared, until his body began to tighten and blood rushed to his groin. That jerked some sense into him, and he turned away with a vicious curse. He downed the rest of the bottle of beer and then splashed some cold water on his face from the kitchen sink.

What the hell was wrong with him? He knew better than to let his guard down, to let personal feelings separate him from good sense. Sydney Wainwright wasn't a woman. She was a job. And he wasn't about to screw himself out of a bundle just because he was horny.

"Luke?"

He pushed away from the sink and turned around. "What?"

At his snarl, she jumped. Her face was scrubbed clean of makeup and she looked young. Innocent. The denim shirt he'd picked up for her was a size small and still a little big on her. "I'm done in the bathroom."

"Good." He glanced around for a place to put her while he showered. "Come here."

She hesitated, her eyes widening slightly, and then she took a step toward him. "What?"

He tested the handle of the refrigerator. Too flimsy. The microwave wouldn't work either. If she had a mind to, she could pick the whole thing up and take off.

He swept a gaze around the rest of the room. "Looks like I'm going to have to tie you to the bedpost."

"Excuse me?"

"While I shower."

"You're going to put the cuffs on me again?" She started rubbing her wrists.

"Did I say that?" His mood had gone south, and he still had one hell of a long week ahead of him. "Get over there."

She cast a sidelong glance at the bed and then looked back at him with those big doe eyes. "Why the bed?"

He pulled out the long red scarf he'd found in the closet. "Move."

She stumbled backward, her fearful gaze fastened on the scarf. "What's that for?"

Luke had a good mind to scare the daylights out of her, but the way she visibly swallowed and the heaving of her chest told him she was frightened enough. "You want me to use this or the cuffs?"

Her face relaxed. "The scarf."

"Then move."

"Look." She pointed to the only kitchen cabinet. "Why can't you use that?"

He shook the handle. It seemed sturdy enough, and unlike the cuffs, the scarf could slip through it. "Okay."

She slowly approached and held out a hand. It shook slightly. He ignored her trembling and grabbed her other hand and wove the scarf between her wrists.

"You're tying them both up?" She tried to pull back.

He tied her to the handle, and then gave an extra tug to be sure the scarf was tight enough. "You think I should leave you a free hand?"

"Just so I can have some water."

"Right." He started unbuttoning his shirt, and her gaze flew to his chest. "You can have all the water you want once I'm through."

"Through?" Her voice cracked.

"With my shower."

"Oh." She leaned a hip against the counter, her relief so plain he almost smiled.

"Sydney?" He lifted her chin with his forefinger.

Her eyes widened.

"Don't think about trying to escape."

She shook her head and jerked away from his touch.

"Good girl." He shrugged out of his shirt. Her gaze immediately went to the undone snap of his Levi's, and she blinked.

Unable to resist, he started unzipping his fly before he turned away. A bright blush filled her cheeks and she quickly averted her eyes.

Laughing, he headed for the bathroom.

Sydney was so angry she almost forgot to breathe. The heat stinging her cheeks no longer had anything to do with embarrassment. She waited until he'd disappeared into the bathroom, and then she started twisting her hands like crazy.

It was no use. He'd tied the scarf too tightly, and she was succeeding only in making her skin raw. She sank against the counter and stared at the open bathroom door. She figured Luke had already gotten into the tub, and if she didn't free herself now, it would be too late. But then she caught his reflection in the mirror.

He was turned toward the tub so she could only see his profile. The unguarded pose fascinated her and she stared with new interest at the thoughtful furrow of his brow as he appeared to be fiddling with something. The showerhead, probably. It hadn't looked as though it had been used in a while.

When he reached up to make an adjustment, Syd got quite a view of his lower chest and stomach, the arrow of hair pointing lower. The same fluttery feeling she'd had earlier returned to her belly. Luke wasn't in any better shape than her personal trainer, but Larry sure never made her feel kind of squishy.

Maybe because Larry was gay.

At least he wasn't a kidnapper.

She shuddered at the reminder, but still kept her gaze trained on Luke as he stepped back and unconsciously rubbed his chest and then his beard-roughened jaw. He leaned toward the mirror to look at his face.

His eyes slowly met hers.

She heard his curse even though his reflection promptly disappeared. Obviously he knew she was watching him. A second later, he came through the door, a white towel wrapped around his hips, thunder in his face.

Sydney tried not to cower. "I wasn't watching you," she said, as he roughly yanked the scarf loose. "I swear I wasn't. I was only—"

She frowned. If she could see him from this position in the kitchen, then he obviously had seen… "You bastard!"

Amusement briefly replaced the scowl on his face, and then he dragged her to the bed and tied one of her wrists to the post. She didn't bother struggling. He'd already tied the knot tighter than necessary, enough to make her skin sting.

He still said nothing, but by the way he clenched his jaw, she knew he was pretty damn angry. Too bad. She wasn't thrilled, either. Who knows how much he saw?

Finally, he stood back. The towel had slipped a little and Sydney had trouble keeping her gaze raised…until he pointed a finger in her face. "Don't move. Not one muscle, or I'll have you trussed tighter than a whore's corset."

She shrunk back and shook her head. "I won't," she whispered, and then waited silently for him to leave.

Her heart still pounded and she tried to calm herself by recalling what he'd said. A whore's corset? What an odd term. Made her wonder about his slight accent again. Maybe he was Cajun, but if so, what did he have to do with the unions in Dallas?

It took her a good minute to realize he'd only tied one of her wrists. Probably because he'd been so angry. Or maybe he thought she was too frightened to try anything. He wouldn't be too far off the mark on that account…if she weren't so desperate.

She rotated her wrist and winced with pain. It didn't matter. She had to try. Slowly, she reached up with her other hand while keeping an eye on the bathroom door. The binding was so tight it was impossible for her to slip even one finger between the fabric.

Finally, after two broken fingernails, she worked her little finger into the knot. Slowly, painfully, with no awareness of how much time passed, she began to loosen it. Twice she had to slow down her breathing and force herself to concentrate. Freedom seemed so close she could almost taste it.

With one more thrust of her finger, the knot loosened and she quickly freed her hand while trying to sit up.

"Shit!"

Her gaze flew toward the bathroom.

Luke stood naked, his tanned body damp and glistening. She sucked in a breath and tried to scramble off the bed. But he was too quick.

He lunged across the mattress, caught her around the waist and flipped her onto her back. And then he swung one of his powerful, muscled legs over her hips and straddled her while he readied the scarf.

His sex lay heavy in the valley between her ribs, half resting against her left breast.

She swallowed, closed her eyes, and prayed.

Chapter Four

Luke cursed under his breath. "Stop it."

Sydney heard every pithy word and slowly opened her eyes, and tried to keep her gaze lifted to his face. "Wh-what?"

"You're shaking so damn hard I can't tie this." He yanked the scarf tight.

She jerked from the pressure. "It isn't my fault."

"The hell it isn't." He glared down at her and when she turned away, used her chin to force her gaze to his. "I told you to cooperate and you wouldn't get hurt."

She blinked and tried not to think about his warm naked flesh pressed against her belly and her breast. "I'm sorry. I—I wasn't trying to get away. I just wanted to get some water."

A humorless smile lifted one side of his mouth. "Right."

She took a shuddering breath, the pressure of his weight making it difficult to breathe deeply. "What are you going to do to me?"

His brows furrowed slightly. Then he eased off, dazedly, almost as if he'd forgotten that he was naked and pinning her to the mattress with his body. "I don't know."

She lowered her lashes. Not that he seemed bothered by his nudity. "I'm sorry," she said, again. "I won't try anything."

"Damn right." He leaned over and cinched the scarf tighter.

She gasped. Not in pain. Semiaroused, his sex brushed her arm, swung perilously close to her face.

"Stay put, Sydney. Or you'll get more than a warning next time." He meaningfully held her gaze for a long, agonizing moment and then let his eyes briefly roam her breasts and hips before turning away and heading back toward the bathroom.

He had a perfectly sculpted backside—like those guys in the beefcake calendars. He either had a lot of time to work out or was into athletics. Of course, not having an honest job allowed time to work out.

She closed her eyes and tried deep, even breathing. Was she going insane? She didn't care about this man's body or how he spent his time. He'd taken her by force. He'd threatened her. She didn't know that he wouldn't harm her. She could cooperate, follow his instruction to the letter, and he could still kill her.

She shivered and drew her knees up to her chest, curling up as best she could, even though her raised arm ached. She blinked, painfully recalling another time she'd claimed this position and refused to get out of bed for three days. She'd finally forced herself up to go to her parents' funeral.

Of course, she'd been hospitalized, banged and broken after the boating accident, but alive. She'd been nineteen, a sophomore at Yale, ready to take on the world, firmly planted in the invincibility of youth. With a jolt, her life had been turned upside down, and she'd ruthlessly learned that no amount of money or privilege could make her immune from pain and suffering.

"What's wrong now?"

She opened her eyes. He stood right in front of her, thankfully in jeans, zipped but not snapped, his chest still bare.

"Nothing," she muttered, closing her eyes again, wishing he'd just go away. Leave her alone for the next week. Assuming he really would let her go then. She sniffed and curled into a tighter ball.

"Sydney?"

She tucked her chin lower.

"Sydney." His voice was closer, and she slowly, cautiously opened her eyes.

He had crouched beside her, at eye level, and she reflexively drew back. His sharp intake of breath made her shrink back as far as her bound hand would let her.

"Look, Sydney, I'm not trying to frighten you." His expression gentled. "And I don't want to hurt you."

"You already have," she said in a small voice that made him flinch.

Abruptly, he stood. "We'll eat in about twenty minutes."

She watched him walk back to the bathroom, her curiosity growing. It hadn't been her imagination. He'd actually flinched. Odd. Maybe he was new at this kidnapping business. Maybe he was having second thoughts about his involvement. Maybe she could...

"Luke?"

He turned around and met her eyes with a hardness that wasn't there a minute ago.

"Never mind."

He said nothing, his gaze staying on her a moment longer, and then he disappeared into the bathroom.

Sydney relaxed against the pillows, her brain and body drained of all energy. What the hell was she going to do? Wait around and hope he didn't kill her? Worse, stay wrapped in the false sense of security that he wouldn't?

Deep down, her every instinct told her this man wouldn't harm her. The belief belied all reason. Was that what her therapist would call denial?

She hadn't seen Rhonda for nearly six months. The psychiatrist had been her lifeline after Syd's parents' death. And then, after the pain of loss eased, she became more of a friend, a confidante. The mother Sydney no longer had.

Willard was great. He'd always been there for her. But he was very much like her father. Concerned with her financial security, with both enjoying and exploiting the Wainwright name. No surprise. They'd been college fraternity brothers, both born into wealth with a talent for compounding their money.

Dr. Rhonda Levine reminded Sydney of her mother, a simple country girl, the daughter of a farmer, who'd caught Harrison Wainwright's eye. Like Sydney's mother, Rhonda had been raised in a middle-class family and understood the struggles of the working class. She'd put herself through school, established her own successful practice and, taking up where Sydney's mother had left off, coached Sydney into self-reliance.

"I have to make a phone call."

At the sound of Luke's voice, she looked up. He'd

pulled on a worn black T-shirt that molded to every muscle in his chest and arms, and showed off his slim waist. But she was more interested in the cell phone he had in his hand.

As if reading her mind, one side of his mouth lifted and he said, "You need the code in order to use it."

"You get an *A* for efficiency."

Ignoring her sarcasm, he ran a hand through his still damp hair. "I'll be right outside the door so give that scheming brain of yours a rest."

"Then it wouldn't matter if you untied me."

He snorted and left.

She kept perfectly still, trying to listen, but all she heard was the creak of the porch floorboards. Followed by several minutes of silence. Which didn't necessarily mean anything. He could be sitting on the steps.

She twisted around to scope out the window and saw him standing near the car, watching her. He continued to talk into the cell phone. Probably reporting in to someone. His partner? Or was Luke just a hired hand? He didn't strike her as a man who'd be content as someone's flunky.

The position was awkward and uncomfortable, and she slumped back against the pillows. Let him stare at her all he wanted. She didn't care. For now. He had to sleep sometime.

The door opened, startling her, and she raised herself on one elbow to watch him enter the cabin and head straight into the small galley kitchen.

"Who'd you call?"

Over his shoulder, he gave her an amused look.

"Your partner?"

Shaking his head, he got something out of the refrigerator. "You're something else."

"Your employer?"

"Enough." Impatience darkened his face.

"Pizza delivery?" she asked quietly, rubbing her bound wrist.

"Don't you ever shut up?" He came around the counter toward her.

She dug her heels into the mattress and scrambled back against the wall. And then she saw that he had a plate in his hand. He stopped to pick up a tray and brought both to her.

"Don't be so jumpy." He tried to hide a smile. The bastard.

She straightened into a sitting position and peered at the plate. Some kind of sandwich made with whole wheat bread and baby gherkins that were her favorite.

"Here." He set the tray down in front of her. "What do you want to drink?"

"Why can't I sit at the table?"

"You have a choice of water, Coke or orange juice."

"Water, please." She stared down at the tray, avoiding his eyes. "I'd really like to eat at the table."

He stayed silent for so long that she finally looked up. He studied her, his brows slightly furrowed, as if considering her request.

"It's not as if I can escape." She gave him her best smile. "You're right here, and I couldn't get far on foot, anyway."

Snickering, he shook his head as he went to the refrigerator and got out a bottle of Evian. Her hope faltered and then resurfaced when he set the water on the table.

"Don't make me regret this," he said as he approached her. "No more chances after this."

She nodded. "I understand."

"I hope so." He jerked the knot loose. "You run again and you stay handcuffed. Period."

She believed him. He looked tired, crankier since the phone call. The scarf fell away from her wrist and she rubbed the offended area. Feeling his gaze on her, she lowered her hand and scooted to the edge of the bed, and then picked up the tray he'd left her and carried it to the table.

After sitting in one of the two chairs, she opened the bottle of water and sipped, her mind racing with possibilities. The call had most likely been made to the people who hired him. If he didn't like what they had to say, maybe she still had a chance of bribing him.

She picked up one of the gherkins and nibbled at it, wondering how to approach the subject without ticking him off, when he came to the table and took the other chair. He'd brought a sandwich and a Coke with him.

He popped the can open and took a big gulp, and then studied his sandwich with a frown. He tore off the top crust before taking a bite.

"You don't like the crust?" she asked.

"Does it look like I do?"

God, he was crabby. She'd only been trying to make conversation. "I just wondered. You made the sandwiches. Why didn't you cut off the crust in the first place?"

He glared at her.

"Never mind." She nibbled more of her gherkin and traced the bottom of the Evian bottle. This obviously was not the way to prep him.

"What's wrong with your sandwich?"

She looked up. He had extraordinary blue eyes. "Nothing."

"You aren't eating." Half of his was already gone.

"I guess I'm not very hungry." She pushed her plate toward him. "Here."

He made a face. "Whole wheat?"

"It won't kill you." She thought for a couple of seconds. "Of course that would solve my problem."

His lips curved in a wry smile. "Think so?"

She sighed. "Don't eat the sandwich. I don't care."

He pushed the plate back at her. "Eat."

"What difference does it make?"

"I don't want you getting sick on me."

"Why? Most kidnap victims don't make it out alive. Right?"

"Jesus." He got up from the table and kicked his chair in.

"Don't go." She bit her lip when he stopped and narrowed his gaze on her. "Sit with me."

He didn't say anything, but after he got another cola out of the fridge, he returned to the table. He glanced at her sandwich. "Sorry it isn't escargot. But eat, dammit."

"I happen to despise escargot." She picked up the sandwich, annoyed at the assumptions some people made about her because she was rich. "And for your information, I don't like champagne or caviar either."

"So?"

"So quit thinking you know so much about me."

He shook his head, took another sip of his cola and then stared out the window, looking bored.

"Luke?"

He shot her a wary glance.

"Now, don't get mad."

His expression hardened.

Obviously the wrong thing to say but she didn't want him jumping up again. "Hear me out, okay?" When he didn't respond, she cleared her throat. "Whatever you're being paid, I can double it."

A slow smile curved one side of his mouth.

"Triple."

He took another sip of his cola.

"Name your price. No police involvement. I give you my word."

Relaxing back in his chair, he stared at her with undisguised amusement, waiting silently, like a cat playing with a mouse.

Anger sparked inside her. "You are doing this for money, aren't you?"

A slight flicker of annoyance in his eyes betrayed his stoic expression.

"I rather doubt you're in this for charity." She hesitated, knowing her temper was rising, knowing his was, as well. "You're working for the union, right?"

He muttered a curse. "Shut up."

"It doesn't matter. Even if you keep me out of the picture past my birthday, I'll still sign the papers once I—" She stopped, the horrid realization sinking in like lead weights.

Swallowing around the sudden lump in her throat, she shivered and looked away, trying to compose herself. Displaying weakness would only give him ammunition. She took a sip of water. Her mouth had dried out, so that she wasn't sure she could speak.

"I promised the employees a share of the company," she said quietly, looking down at her folded hands. "They've all worked hard for Wainwright Corporation, some of them for half their lives. They deserve more than a paycheck and the occasional bonus. You can kill me, but it won't stop the buyout." She lifted her gaze. "I've already made provisions for—"

She stopped when their eyes met. He had the most peculiar look. Confusion and anger and mistrust all fused together in an alarming expression. She picked up the Evian again, ignoring the tremble in her fingers.

"I'm not going to kill you," he said in a low, quiet voice.

"How can I believe you?"

He didn't say anything. Just stared at her. "Guess you can't."

LUKE WAITED until she was in the bathroom before he made another call. This time he'd let her close the door. While outside on the cell phone earlier he'd checked the bathroom window. It was small and although it would be a tight squeeze, she could probably maneuver her way out, but not without the splintered wood and cracked glass doing some bodily damage. It wouldn't be easy and he'd know if she tried escaping through there.

She'd try of course. She was tenacious, that one. But he'd been warned about her feistiness and quick thinking. In fact, he knew a lot about her. How she'd graduated at the top of her class from Yale, how she had gotten involved with her father's company at an age when most young women were more interested in making the social scene.

Good for her. She was ambitious. All the better to make more money. Luke knew that kind, too. Loaded to the gills but always wanting more. Multiple homes. Garages full of expensive cars. More money than common sense. And never satisfied.

Yet, she'd talked about selling the company to the employees. What was that about?

None of his business. He didn't even want to know.

Damn, he was sorry he'd gotten into this mess. Normally he took simple jobs. More short-term and straightforward. Pissed him off that she was right. The money had been too good to turn down.

Keeping an eye on the door, he stepped out onto the porch and hit Speed Dial on his phone. For the second time in two hours he got voice mail. He left another message and then called his own voice mail. Nothing.

He slid the phone back into his pocket and gazed off at the northern horizon. Looked as if it were raining in Dallas, which meant they'd get it next. Good. That might give her second thoughts about trying to escape. Although she was different, that one. Not like some of the other rich, pampered women he'd had the misfortune to tangle with. They always paid well, though. And right now money was important—if he wanted to make it to Brazil.

He tapped his breast pocket, looking for a pack of cigarettes. But he'd quit. Did so two months after he'd gotten out of the joint. Withdrawal had been a challenge, but fortunately he'd never cared much for the filthy habit. There just hadn't been a lot to do in prison. Ironically, he'd had time to work out and had gotten into the best shape of his life, while polluting his lungs at the same time.

He heard a noise from inside the cabin. He stayed on the porch, but got closer to the door so Sydney would see him and know this was not the time to make a run for it. It would piss him off to have to chase her down and end up getting rained on and muddy.

He watched her leave the bathroom, stop and look around. She spotted him and her chin immediately went up as she sauntered unhurriedly to the table as if she were the Queen of Sheba. She was something, all right. Pulling that gun on him. Someone was going to have to teach her how to use the damn thing before she got herself killed.

He patted his pocket again, muttered a curse and then got the cell phone out and hit Speed Dial. He started to move off the porch for privacy, but he got voice mail again.

Something was wrong. Nothing he could pinpoint, but he felt the bad vibes deep in his gut. Paranoia, probably. So the guy wasn't answering his cell phone. A bad connection maybe, or it needed a charge.

In the distance, he thought he heard thunder. A second later, the sound boomed overhead, like a bowling ball slamming the pins. Lightning flashed in the darkening sky.

He glanced inside. Sydney sat at the table, clutching her bottle of water, her eyes wide with surprise. She didn't seem frightened, just startled. Probably annoyed that the weather had ruined her escape plans.

Good. He tucked the cell phone back into his jeans just as the first onslaught of rain started. Large hard drops pelted his left arm where it stuck out past the overhang. He jerked it back in and turned to watch the downpour.

Another clap of thunder shook the porch's rickety railing, even rattled the window panes. He sure hoped there weren't any leaks in the roof. He hadn't used the place in three years.

He'd gotten to the door when he heard it. The sound mimicked thunder. But it was a gunshot.

Chapter Five

"What was that noise?" Sydney asked when Luke came in.

"Thunder."

"No, the other noise."

He turned off one of the lights, leaving only a dim lamp on, and glanced out the window, pretty much confirming her suspicion. "I only heard thunder."

She smiled to herself. He was a good liar but she knew what she'd heard. A car backfiring. Which meant someone was close enough for her to seek help.

He studied his watch, his expression sober, a tic at his jaw belying his apprehension. Apparently doing more than calculating the time, he frowned in concentration, his face darkening. Finally, he said, "We'll be leaving in about an hour."

"You're kidding."

"Get your things ready."

"But it's pouring and it'll be pitch-black by then."

He didn't answer, only got out the cell phone, but this time he didn't step outside to use it. He punched a couple of buttons, waited with the phone to his ear, cursed and then put the phone back into his pocket.

"Where are we going?" she asked, an emerging fear taking hold as she watched him check her gun and then stick it back into the waistband of his jeans.

"Pack up the food. The sacks are in the cabinet under the sink." He picked up his small duffel bag and jammed in some T-shirts he'd unpacked earlier. "And don't turn on any more lights."

She got up from the table. "Tell me where we're going."

"You'll find out when we get there." His voice was sharp, his expression hard, and she stayed quiet as she did as he asked.

Someone had to know she was missing by now. Maybe they'd called the police, started a search party. Maybe now was the time she should make a run for it.

No, it was too soon for the police to have tracked her to such a remote place. But the woods were dense and probably filled with game. There could be hunters camping out there. They'd help her.

"Get your clothes together when you're done. Anything not packed in twenty minutes gets left behind."

It wasn't as if she had much. Just the few things he'd given her. She continued to load the bags with cans of cashews and peanuts and tuna, a couple of boxes of crackers, half a jar of peanut butter.

He brought the cooler close to the refrigerator and started storing the milk and butter and packages of cheese, mostly Gouda and Camembert, which she usually loved but which made her stomach roll watching him.

She wished he'd say something. Anything. His sudden furtiveness made her nervous. Obviously, something had gone wrong with his plan. But was it to her advantage?

The rain hadn't eased. It bombarded the roof with drops big enough that it almost sounded like hail. If she screamed, it wouldn't do any good. Any hope of escape meant she had to make a run for it.

Luke abruptly looked up at her and stared, as if reading her mind. Their eyes met, briefly, and then she went back to loading the bag.

"Don't even think about it."

She glanced up, her eyebrows raised in innocence. "What?"

"It's muddy and slippery and you wouldn't make it ten feet."

"I have no idea what you're talking about." She put the last can in the plastic bag and tied the handle into a knot, refusing to look up again.

He didn't say anything, just continued to load the cooler. She darted him a look. His jaw was set, his expression grim. He raised himself from his crouched position and instantly looked toward the window.

"I don't know what you did with the bag you gave me," she said, hoping he'd stay preoccupied.

"It's near the bed."

She knew exactly where it was and hurried over and kicked the canvas bag under the bed before he turned around. "Where?" she asked, pretending to search.

He'd taken out his cell phone and, with an impatient sigh he took several long strides toward the bed. She inched backward toward the door. As soon as he crouched to look under the bed, she turned and ran.

She heard a pithy four-letter word, and before she

could turn the latch, he grabbed her around the waist. She tried to jerk away but he pulled her against him, her back pressed hard to his chest, and then he caught one of her wrists.

"You stupid little fool. You want to get yourself killed?" His grip tightened, and she whimpered.

"Ironic, coming from you." She twisted her hand and although he wouldn't release her, he slackened his punishing hold.

She managed to move away and turn around. Indecision flickered in his eyes and he started to speak, but then closed his mouth again and shook his head.

His grip again tightened for an instant, as if reminding her who was in control, and then he released her. "I didn't want to have to tie you up again."

"Please don't," she said, her voice catching.

"Right."

She rubbed her wrist where he'd held her. "I wasn't trying to run away."

He herded her toward the bed and picked up the scarf. "It's dark enough. We'll leave now."

"That really isn't necessary." She hid her hands behind her back.

He snorted. "I'll tie them like that."

"No." Reluctantly, she crossed her wrists in front of her. While he wrapped the scarf around them, something occurred to her, and her gaze drifted toward the window. Not that she could see outside. He'd shut the blinds. "Why does it have to be dark for us to leave?"

He gave the scarf a final tug. "Stay put."

"What about my things? I haven't packed them yet."

"Sydney." He made her name a warning.

She gave him a curt nod, and then watched him search for and locate her bag, gather the clothes and toiletries. He didn't fold anything, just stuffed the jeans and shorts and cotton shirts inside.

After he was finished, he carried both their bags and the grocery items to the door.

He gave her an assessing look. "Come here."

"Why?"

"Now."

She didn't have much choice. She moved closer but froze when she saw the handcuffs. "I thought you wouldn't use them again."

"Just while I load the car." He pulled her closer and snapped a cuff around one wrist.

"I'm already tied up."

He forced her into the kitchen and locked the other cuff around the refrigerator door handle.

"Come on, Luke, please don't—"

He cut her off by shoving a bandana in her mouth.

LUKE DIDN'T USE the lights as he slowly drove the car down the dirt road. The sky had cleared some and enough moonlight guided him. If someone were out there, he hoped like hell there wasn't so much illumination that they'd spot the black Town Car.

He probably was being paranoid, overly cautious. At least, he hoped that's all it was. The gunshots could have belonged to an amateur hunter, too stupid to be out in the woods, let alone in possession of a loaded rifle. But he'd had enough bullets whiz by him to know it had come close. Too close for his comfort.

He'd fired one shot back. High enough that it

wouldn't do any damage but still serve as a warning that he was armed and ready to react. He figured that if anyone were after them, they'd lay low until morning. Give him and Sydney enough time to get lost.

Better to err on the side of caution. They could always return to the cabin if he felt it was safe. Tonight, they'd get on the highway and stay in a motel if he got too tired to drive. If they were being followed, he'd know it.

He checked the rearview mirror and stared into the darkness. No one in sight. Which didn't mean squat.

He patted his pocket and swore. It would be damn hard to pass up the Marlboros at the next convenience store.

And here he thought this would be a cushy job. A time to catch up on the Patterson and King novels he didn't seem to have time for since getting out of the joint.

At least with Sydney gagged and trussed up like a Thanksgiving turkey in the backseat, it was blessedly silent. Of course, once he removed the gag she'd be squawking like a wet hen.

He chased all thoughts of her out of his mind. Too dangerous. He had to concentrate on his driving. It was hard enough with no headlights. The two shallow ruts from traffic heading back into the woods helped guide the tires, but he had to pay attention so that they didn't end up with a tree for a hood ornament.

Five minutes later, they reached a short paved road leading to the highway. No streetlights yet. But without the trees blocking the moon, visibility was much better. Another five minutes and they'd reach the highway, ten minutes after that, the interstate. He'd breathe easier then.

SYDNEY BLINKED at the bright light shining into the car window, penetrating the heavy black tinted glass as if it were plastic wrap. How could she possibly have fallen asleep?

Her wrists and ankles still bound, she struggled to sit upright, amazed that she could have fallen asleep at all. She'd been too afraid and angry. But drained, too. Blinking again, she prayed this was just a nightmare. But she wasn't lounging in her cherry sleigh bed, wrapped in cream satin sheets with three extra pillows.

Across the empty parking lot, a gaudy neon pink motel sign flashed in front of her, below it, the word Vacancy in red. She peered over to see if Luke was lying across the front seat. A small duffel bag sat in the passenger seat. That was it.

She scanned the parking lot, paying close attention to the lighted area with the office sign. He was nowhere in sight. Had he gotten a room and left her in the car? Doubtful. She tried the door, not surprised to find it locked.

Her left leg cramped and she winced, the taste of the bandana bitter on her lips. She tried to swallow but her mouth was too dry. How could he have left her tied up like this with no water? To make matters worse, she had to go to the bathroom so badly that in another ten minutes it wouldn't be pretty.

The door opened suddenly, startling her. Luke stood there, his gaze briefly touching her before he surveyed the dark parking lot, and then he ducked his head in, his face coming close to hers, his eyes issuing a fierce warning.

"I've got us a room," he said, grasping her chin when she tried to turn away. "The place is nearly empty, and the owner is half-deaf. If you try anything, no one will help you, but I promise you will regret it."

She glared back.

"Understand?"

She gave a curt nod.

"I'm going to untie your ankles and then we'll walk to the room. It's not far, right behind the car."

She mumbled into the gag, asking him to remove it.

Apparently he understood her garbled attempt, and shook his head. "Maybe after we get inside." He moved back and straightened, and then glanced around. "Come on."

With him holding her arm, she scooted across the seat, cringing when her leg muscles cramped in protest. Suddenly, it occurred to her that she might not be able to stand. No telling how many hours they'd driven while she'd been tied up.

She swung her legs to the ground and tried to stand. Luke slid his hand from her upper arm to her elbow to help support her, but as soon as she used all her weight, her knees buckled. He caught her around the waist, holding her tight against his warm body and she sagged into him with relief.

"I know you're tired," he whispered. "Let's get inside and you'll have a nice soft bed to sleep on."

She nodded and let him help her to the orange door marked with a big gold *Six* directly behind the car. He didn't use the key he had in his hand. The door was already unlocked.

The room was small and a little shabby, but looked clean. More importantly, there were two beds. On one of them, he'd already placed their bags.

Her legs still shaky, she hobbled toward the other bed and he kept abreast of her, his arm tucked snugly around her waist. She felt completely safe, knowing instinctively he wouldn't let her fall.

In the next instant, anger and resentment welled inside her. Where the hell was the gratitude she felt coming from? He'd kidnapped her, taken her against her will, scared the daylights out of her. He wasn't her friend. He didn't want to help her. The disgust she felt for herself injected her with renewed energy and she jerked away from him.

He lowered his hands, his gaze probing. "I assume you want to go to the bathroom before you go to bed."

Her only response was to turn around and head for the bathroom door. She automatically left it open, not ready to go another round with him. But she angled the door for maximum privacy.

She did her business, awkwardly with her bound hands, while listening for his movements. It sounded as if he was unpacking.

"Sydney?"

She quickly finished pulling down her skirt.

"I have your cosmetic bag with your toothbrush and toothpaste." It suddenly appeared dangling from the end of his arm. He stayed back, though.

She grabbed it, roughly, out of his hand, and then walked out of the bathroom, catching him by the shirt when he started to leave.

He turned abruptly, his gaze narrowed.

She pointed to the gag.

He hesitated, started to reach for the knot he'd made at her nape, and then stopped. "One sound out of you and I'll leave the damn thing on for the entire week. Got it?"

She nodded.

He held up a warning finger. "I mean it, Sydney."

Frustrated, a growling sound came from her throat.

The corners of his mouth twitched. "Okay, I'm trusting you."

Trusting *her?* She did everything she could to keep from rolling her eyes. Instead she waited calmly for him to remove the bandana.

As soon as it was away from her mouth, she said, "How could you keep me tied up and gagged and left in the car that way? Do you—"

He clamped a hand over her mouth. "What part of shut up don't you understand?"

She reared her head back and managed to free herself of his hand. "I didn't even raise my voice."

He pushed his face close to hers, his eyes angry, the veins on his neck bulging. "I don't want to hear from you at all."

Sydney tried not to shrink back and moistened her parched lips. "I—I was thirsty."

He blinked, and she could've sworn she saw regret flicker in his eyes. "I'll get you some water."

"My hands?" she asked, holding them up. Her wrists had started to throb a few hours ago. Now they were just numb.

"Look, I'm too exhausted to run."

After a long assessing look, he shook his head and then fumbled with the scarf, mumbling, "You're way too much trouble. I have a good mind to cut you loose."

"What?"

He gave her the briefest glance while pulling the scarf free and then he turned away.

"What did you say?"

"Forget it." He pulled his cell phone out and waited, looking pointedly at her. "Get in the bathroom before I gag you again."

She started to insist he explain about cutting her loose, but he looked angry and frustrated, and she didn't doubt he would bind and gag her again. She'd bring it up later. Maybe the job wasn't what he'd anticipated and she could bribe him with enough money to return her to Dallas.

Slipping back into the bathroom, she angled the door again, and then turned on the shower. God, it felt as if it had been a week since she had a bath instead of just this morning.

She checked her watch.

Three-twenty?

They'd been traveling for hours. Where were they? She glanced over her shoulder and then peeked out the small window over the sink. The area looked pretty rural but no clues as to what part of Texas they were in…or even if they were still in Texas.

She shivered, tested the water and turned the knob to make the shower hotter. Quickly, she stripped and got in the stall, pulling the curtain shut. She hadn't even brought fresh clothes in with her but she didn't care. The warm water felt good on her bruised wrists and ankles. If only she had a tub to soak in with the scented bath salts Willard had given her last week.

Willard… He had to be frantic by now. And Rick, too. God, why hadn't she listened to them? Why had she been so stubborn? She'd thought she was so damn independent. Tears welled in her eyes.

Dammit! She wouldn't cry. She had to keep her wits about her. She had to be able to…

Luke banged on the door. "Hurry up. We have to get some sleep."

She clutched the shower curtain like a shield, but he went away, and she breathed a sigh of relief. Not that she was afraid of him, which was truly odd. Maybe it was denial. Maybe she'd finally gone crazy. Or maybe she was suffering from Stockholm syndrome, the same bizarre thing Patty Hearst had encountered. But she didn't think he meant to harm her. It was the people he worked for that scared her. Mostly because he seemed so apprehensive.

After letting the water sluice over her tired muscles for another minute, she turned off the shower and rubbed herself dry. She picked up her clothes but, loath to put the same thing back on, she secured the towel around her and went to the door, leaving it angled so that she could poke her face out.

Luke, obviously having anticipated her needs, had left her bag on the floor just outside the door. He was sitting on the bed his back to her, talking on the cell phone. She froze and tried to listen, but his voice was too low. He disconnected the call, muttered a curse and threw the cell phone on the bed.

Taking her bag, she quietly slipped back into the bathroom. She pulled on a pair of running shorts and a T-shirt, and then slathered moisturizer over her freshly scrubbed face. The brief and absurd thought that she didn't want Luke to see her without makeup really annoyed her.

She stuffed everything back into the bag and then opened the door.

The beds had been pushed together.

Chapter Six

Luke turned suddenly. "How long have you been standing there?"

She stared at the joined beds. "Why did you do that?"

He grabbed the cell phone and stuck it in his pocket, and then eyed her speculatively for a moment. "Have you called anyone?"

"I haven't been out of your sight, remember?"

Ignoring her sarcasm, he shook his head and stared off toward the ugly orange curtains, his thoughts clearly far away. Finally he said, "We need to get some sleep. We'll leave in four or five hours."

"Why did you push the beds together?"

"Either that, or I tie you to the headboard. Your choice."

She toyed with the hem of her shirt, trying to see the logic, but not wanting to irritate him. He was in a strange mood—kind of edgy, angry, restless. Harder. "What's the difference?"

"I'm a light sleeper. You try to leave, and I'll know."

She hesitated, tempted to argue, but then another thought occurred to her. "Why do we have to leave in five hours?"

"No more questions." He got his bag and went to the bathroom, leaving the door open.

She glanced at the entry door, which was deadbolted, of course, and where he'd also strategically placed a chair to make escape both difficult and noisy.

He appeared with his toothbrush already covered with toothpaste. He didn't say anything, just made a point of checking on her.

Casually, she walked toward the bed. Out of the corner of her eye, she saw him duck back into the bathroom. Her gaze flew to the nightstand. No phone. The table near the window didn't have one either.

"Looking for this?"

She turned around to find his mouth curved in a cocky grin. In his hand was the old-fashioned yellow phone. Never had she wanted so much to slap someone across the face.

"Actually, I was looking for the remote control," she said, poking around the crowded nightstand and making a show of looking for the remote.

"No television. Get some sleep."

"Excuse me?"

"You heard me." He went back to the bathroom, leaving her to seethe over his high-handedness over something so trivial.

Knowing she couldn't make it out the door, she went to the opposite side of the window so he couldn't accuse her of trying to escape and looked out at the parking lot. Besides the Town Car, only one other vehicle was parked across the lot. Luke was right. Even if she screamed, she doubted anyone would hear, and then her captivity would only become worse.

"Shut the damn curtain."

At the harshness of his voice, she jumped. She turned around just as he pulled off his shirt. She stared at his chest, her feminine appreciation of the tautly curved muscles defining his pecs making her grow warm. "I wasn't doing anything."

"Then don't do anything with the damn curtains shut." He flung his shirt onto a chair and then unbuckled his belt.

Sydney blinked. Surely he didn't plan to strip right in front of her.

"If you're waiting for a show, it's over." He pulled off his belt and sent it flying the way of his shirt. Then he picked up one of the pillows and punched it into shape.

She cleared her throat. "May I turn up the air conditioner?"

"You're hot?"

"I like to sleep under the covers."

Sighing, he pointed to the ancient wall unit. "Go ahead."

She tucked a strand of hair behind her ear, still unfamiliar with the shorter cut. "Where are we going?" she asked as she fiddled with the control switches. It made a loud banging noise.

Luke took several angry strides across the room and pulled her hand away from the knob. "What are you trying to do?"

She shrunk away from him. "Nothing. I was just trying to figure out how to work it."

He made the necessary adjustment and then turned on her. "Ah, that's right. A rich girl like you wouldn't know how to do anything so simple."

"You don't know anything about me," she said, glaring, her temper sparked.

"Don't be so sure."

"You only know what you want to believe."

"Get in bed." He yawned and stretched, his belly so flat that his jeans gaped.

She looked away. "Guess I hit a nerve."

"Right."

It made her angrier that she couldn't seem to provoke him. "I think I'd rather you separate the beds and tie me to the headboard."

He frowned, and then a slow grin tugged at his mouth. "You think I want to play hide-the-salami with you?"

His meaning took a moment to register, and then heat stung her cheeks. "You're so crude."

His smile broadened. "Don't worry, sweetheart." His gaze roamed her body. "You aren't my type."

"Screw you."

His eyebrow lifted, and he laughed. "If you insist, I could make an exception."

Lifting her chin, she tried to pull one of the beds apart.

He closed a hand around her arm, any trace of humor gone. "Get in bed."

She had the strangest and most inappropriate reaction to his touch, and she did as she was told so she could hide under the covers. He turned off the overhead light, but left the one on in the bathroom, angling the door to diffuse the illumination.

A moment later, she heard him climb into the bed next to her. Because of the separate frames, the mattress didn't dip and she wondered how he thought he'd know if she were to slip out of bed. She found out when he threw an arm over her. Jerking, she gave a small yelp and he drew her closer.

"Do that again and I'll tie you up *and* gag you." His mouth was so close his minty breath stirred her hair. In a lower voice, he added, "Sleep well."

Right. She stared at the ceiling, embarrassed and curious about how her body was reacting to him. How could she have the slightest attraction? He was holding her against her will, both figuratively and literally. It didn't make sense that for a brief moment she'd wanted to snuggle against his chest.

She bit down on her lip and closed her eyes. How could less than twenty-four hours have passed since her entire world had been turned upside down? She was supposed to have attended a board meeting last night. She should be showing off her new haircut and highlights. Planning tomorrow night's dinner party so she could introduce Julie to Rick.

A tear slipped from her eye and slid into her hair. She sniffed and rolled over onto her side under Luke's heavy arm. Briefly he tensed, and then relaxed again, his arm still anchored around her waist. Facing the wall, she felt another tear escape and closed her eyes tight.

Almost as if he'd sensed her distress, he tightened his arm around her. Not in a threatening way, but more a gesture of comfort. Which was absurd. Even if he did know she was upset, he didn't care about her. She was simply a commodity, a meal ticket. Willard would pay any amount asked for her return.

She couldn't think about Willard and Rick and her brand-new bed in her newly decorated apartment right now. She had to sleep, get rested enough to keep her wits about her. Luke was bound to make a mistake. One that would allow her to escape.

She yawned, and Luke shifted so that she lay back against his chest. His breathing had already grown heavy. Within a minute, she sank into peaceful oblivion.

"SYDNEY."

Not even an eyelash flickered.

"Sydney." Bending over her, he gently touched her arm.

She made a soft sound of protest and tried to roll over, but he wouldn't let her. He shook her shoulder and waited for her to open her eyes.

"Sydney, you have to get up. Now." The harshness in his voice prompted her eyes wide open. Not the way he'd wanted to wake her, but if that's what it took…

She blinked, gave him a confused look, and then pulled the covers up to her chin.

"You have to get up. We're leaving in fifteen minutes."

"What time is it?" She yawned and covered her mouth.

"It doesn't matter."

"I see you're a morning person," she mumbled and reluctantly drew back the covers. Before she sat up, she raised her arms above her head and stretched. Her shirt rode up just high enough to expose her navel, the way her waist dipped in and her hips flared.

He looked away and took a sip of the instant coffee he'd made. It tasted nasty. The water out of the tap hadn't been hot enough, but the caffeine was doing the trick. Bringing him out of the fog.

"There's stuff for a cup of coffee in the bathroom. It isn't great, but we'll stop somewhere along the way." He carried his bag to the door and then moved the curtain a fraction and glanced outside. No cars in the parking lot. Good.

"Where are we going?"

"What difference does it make?"

She'd swung her feet to the floor and then just sat there staring at him. "I don't know."

"Then get ready." The truth was he didn't know where they were headed. His entire plan had been shot to hell.

They were supposed to stay in the cabin for a week to ten days. No one knew where they were supposed to be. Except the person who hired him. Of course, someone could've been following Sydney when he picked her up and followed them to the cabin. Maybe the shot had been just a warning. Not that he could take the chance.

"It's not too late to take me back," she said in a small voice. "You could be rid of me and still make some money."

He looked at his watch. "Now you have twelve minutes."

She headed for the bathroom, but then stopped at the door. "Or you could just leave me here. You wouldn't have to drive all the way back to Dallas. I'd make sure the money we agreed upon got to you. You'd have my word."

He turned away from the pleading in her eyes. He should tell her the truth. This kind of job wasn't his thing. Even before he'd agreed to take it on, he knew it was foolish. Shit. The money had blinded him. "Right."

"Luke? Wait."

He spared her a glance and then went to the curtain

and looked out onto the parking lot. Although he was pretty sure they hadn't been followed, he wasn't taking any chances.

"I know you think I'm being naive because you don't know me, but if I give my word there'll be no police involvement and the money sent anywhere you want—" She sighed. "You're right. That sounds ridiculous. How about if I arrange for the money to be wired right now? You'll have it in your hands and you just walk away."

He grunted. "You now have ten minutes."

She made a sound of frustration and then disappeared into the bathroom.

Luke pulled out his cell phone. She had spunk, and she was certainly no prima donna. Tenacious little thing. She didn't seem sheltered and spoiled as he had expected. Of course the fact that she handled her own transportation, be it a cab or driving herself, told him a lot. He knew now it hadn't been out of rebellion but simple independence. He kind of liked her.

Maybe he should tell her the truth. God knew she deserved it. But he couldn't ignore the possibility that knowing the truth could get her killed.

SYDNEY FINISHED brushing her teeth and hair. Something had shifted in Luke. He seemed more preoccupied, more uncertain. If she had any hope of negotiating, now was the time. She had to watch herself, though, not get too pushy or desperate. Calm, simple logic was her best approach.

She heard him moving around, pulling the beds apart, and gathering the few things he'd brought inside.

When she thought she heard the door, she ducked her head out. The door was open and he was rummaging through the trunk.

He stood only a couple of yards away. She wouldn't be able to make a run for it. But she should be able to do something… Her gaze drew to the yellow phone. He'd returned it to the nightstand.

Her heart thudded. This could be her only opportunity. With no time to waste, she held her breath and moved slowly enough not to attract attention, one eye on Luke. She made it past the open door and crouched between the beds. Her mind raced as she picked up the receiver and dialed.

Willard would have been her first choice. He'd always handled everything, even when her father was alive, but it was early Saturday morning and Willard always played golf with Rick. Assuming neither of them had discovered she was missing yet. Since she had time for only one call, Jeff was her best bet. He was a late sleeper.

It rang four times. Once more, and she knew the answering machine would pick it up. She'd never prayed so hard in her life.

"Hello?"

Sydney blinked at the familiar sounding voice. It sounded an awful lot like Julie. But that couldn't be…

"Hello," the woman said again, this time in a sing-song voice. "Last chance."

Sydney was too stunned to answer.

Julie added, "You snooze you lose," and then hung up.

Sydney dropped the phone back into the cradle. What the hell was her hairdresser doing at Jeff's house?

LUKE TOOK one last look around before closing the trunk. They hadn't been followed, of that he was quite certain, and the temptation to stay where they were was great. Except if the motel got any more guests, he'd lose control of Sydney. He didn't want to have to bind and gag her again, which meant they needed someplace more isolated.

The whirring sound of a helicopter drew his attention. Shading his eyes against the rising sun, he looked up. The bird was flying low. It wasn't military or police issue, but private as far as he could tell, possibly belonging to a local rancher. Some of the bigger ranches used choppers for herding cattle, as well as for their own personal transportation into Dallas or Houston. Still, it bothered him that it would be flying around out here in the boonies.

He entered the room, closing the door behind him and saw the top of Sydney's head between the beds. The same instant he heard the receiver hit the cradle he realized the phone wasn't on the nightstand.

"Shit!" He came around the bed and grabbed her arm. "What the hell are you doing?"

She looked blankly at him.

He jerked her to her feet. "Sydney, who did you call?"

"No one."

"Tell me who you called." His grip on her arm tightened, and she flinched. He eased up. This was his fault. How could he have been so damn stupid?

She just shook her head,

"Did you call the police?"

Again, she shook her head, the expression on her face an odd mixture of misery and confusion.

"Look," he said, calmly, "I'm not going to jump down your throat. But it's important I know who you called and what you told them."

"No one answered," she said, sniffing. "I mean, she answered but I didn't say anything. I just hung up."

"Who's she?"

"A woman." She gazed up at him with sad eyes. "I called the guy I've been seeing and a woman answered." Her gaze darted away, but not before he saw the humiliation lurking in her eyes.

"Did you say anything at all to her?"

"No." Her voice sharpened as anger replaced hurt.

He let her go and picked up the last small bag. Damn, he hoped she was telling the truth. No matter, they'd be long gone soon. "We have to get going."

She sighed.

He took a final look around, assuring himself nothing had been left behind, and then his gaze came to rest on her. She paid him no attention, just stared off, nibbling her lower lip. "I'm sorry about your boyfriend," he said gruffly.

"He isn't my boyfriend. I'd only been seeing him a couple of months." She pushed back her hair and straightened her shoulders. "The stupid jerk."

Luke squelched a smile as he took her arm. "I agree."

She darted him a wary look.

"Oh, yeah." He stopped at the door. "If you pull a stunt like that again, I will keep you tied up. Period. No discussion. Understand?"

She lifted a shoulder in indifference, her sudden lack of spirit oddly disappointing him.

"Don't say a word until we get in the car," he warned.

"I won't," she said meekly.

Just as he turned the doorknob, she put on the brakes and he looked sharply at her.

"Did he hire you?" she asked, the fire back in her eyes.

"Who?"

"Jeff's representing the union, isn't he?"

"I have no idea who you're talking about."

Her shoulders sagged. "You wouldn't tell me if he was the one."

"Probably not." He thought for a moment and added, "Look, I honestly never heard of this guy Jeff."

She stared at Luke with mistrust. "I guess the same person who hired you could have hired him."

"I doubt it," he murmured.

"Why?" She stared pensively at him.

"Let's go." He'd said too much. Although the way things were going, he'd have to tell her the truth soon. Still, all he had was a suspicion. Certainly not enough to betray his employer.

Not that Sydney would believe him anyway. From what he knew of her sheltered, cushioned life, he doubted she'd tasted the bitterness of betrayal. That allowed for some strong denial. He understood the process all too well. Too bad he hadn't wised up before he'd landed in prison.

"Luke?" She gave a small shrug and avoided his eyes. "Thanks for what you said."

He nodded and gave her elbow a light squeeze. "Ready?"

"Do I have a choice?"

Good. Her fight was back. "Remember, we go straight to the car. No talking or stopping." He opened the door and, using the remote control, unlocked the car doors.

The helicopter had stayed in the area. He couldn't see it, but it had gotten considerably louder. Uneasy, he rushed Sydney to the car, opened the back door and urged her inside. He turned around to see the chopper hovering above the woods behind the motel.

He went around the back and opened the driver's side, trying like hell to look unconcerned. No reason to panic yet. Those guys could have a perfectly legitimate reason for being out there. Maybe hunting. Or tracking stray cattle.

His gut told him otherwise. He threw the bag onto the passenger seat and then hesitated before climbing behind the wheel, pretending to search his pockets. He slid the chopper a furtive glance. Two men inside. The passenger wore camouflage fatigues. Luke couldn't be sure, but he thought he saw the butt of a rifle.

The possibility was enough for him. He got in the car, his mind racing. If he remembered correctly, there was nothing but woods and highway for the next sixty or seventy miles. Not much traffic, a few trucks pulling horse trailers or sometimes a big rig headed for the coast.

He eased onto the highway at normal speed. In a few minutes, he'd know if the guys in the chopper were following them. If they were, shit, he had no idea what he should do next. Except to get the hell out of sight. Or, if he was lucky, a well-aimed shot could bring the sucker down.

And then he'd have to have a painful talk with Sydney.

Chapter Seven

Sydney twisted around to look at the helicopter flying low behind them. Too low for her peace of mind…unless it was a police or FBI helicopter, but it wasn't noted anywhere on the sleek black body.

"Luke?"

"Keep your head down."

"But—"

"Sydney, please." His gaze darted to the rearview mirror, briefly touching her, and then went to the helicopter. "I have some explaining to do, but it's going to have to wait. In the meantime, you've got to keep out of sight."

Indecision overwhelmed her. Why should she believe him? If it were the police, of course he'd want her to keep out of sight.

The car sped up and she clutched the leather armrest. In the movies, the police used some sort of megaphone to warn the driver of a car to stop. Whoever was in the helicopter hadn't identified themselves, and the way they flew low along the highway wasn't prudent. Dangerous, actually. Maybe Luke was right. Maybe…

A loud bang. Sounded like a gunshot.

The car swerved sharply.

Sydney screamed.

"Keep your head down," Luke shouted.

She dove to the floor.

Another gunshot. Sydney covered her ears as the metal groaned with the hit. The car swerved again.

"Sydney! You okay?"

"Yes."

"It's going to get bumpy. Hold on."

He took a sharp right and Sydney fell against the door, feeling the jolt the instant they left the pavement and hit the rocky ground. The car bumped and dipped. Tree branches scraped the side of the doors.

Her knee made violent contact with the metal footrest, and she bit her lip to keep from crying out from the pain. Underneath the car, shrubs scraped the bottom, making a horrible grating noise. The helicopter stayed close overhead, the thunderous whirring vibrating in her ears and making her teeth chatter.

"Okay, Sydney?"

"Fine."

"We're going to stop and—"

"No, we can't. We have to keep going. The helicopter is right above us."

"Listen to me."

Sydney swallowed the panic blocking her throat. The car sank into a rut and then bounced out. "What?"

"I'm going to get out. I want you to stay here. Keep your head down."

"No, you can't! What are you going to do? You can't go up against a—"

"Don't argue, Sydney. You have to trust me. It's our only chance."

Trust him? Hysterical laughter bubbled in her chest. She squeezed her eyes shut. "Okay."

Her head bumped the door handle as he made a sudden turn and then stopped the car. "You have to stay down," he said, and before she could object, he jumped out.

She did as he asked, but after a minute of listening to the whirring of the helicopter blades and not knowing what was happening, she couldn't stand it. Slowly, she raised her head by inches so that her eyes were just level with the top of the car seat.

A thicket of trees surrounded the car. Broken branches lay across the windshield and the hood. The bumper of the car had missed a massive oak trunk by inches.

At first, she couldn't see Luke and alarm rose in her throat. But then she saw him, standing under a tree, perfectly still, his feet shoulder-length apart, his gun aimed toward a patch of blue sky between the trees.

A second later, he fired.

She put her hands over her ears and ducked, but not before she heard the whirring falter.

Another shot, this time the sound muffled by her hands. She jerked back the car's sunroof and, through a clearing in the trees, saw the helicopter drop a few feet, the body lurching before the pilot righted it. Swaying, it grazed the treetops, the blades sputtering, making the helicopter pitch forward.

Engine laboring, it pulled up again, barely missing the treetops before it flew off. From the sound it had taken a serious hit. It wouldn't be returning. At least, not any time soon.

Shivering, Sydney cautiously opened the car door. She couldn't see Luke. Panic slithered down her spine. She'd heard two shots. Had Luke fired them both? Or had the second one come from the helicopter?

Had Luke been shot?

The sudden thought rocked her right to her core. She shouldn't care. That would set her free.

"Luke!"

No answer. The whir of the helicopter faded in the distance.

She got out and cupped her shaking hands around her mouth. "Luke!"

Eerie silence followed. No wind. Not even a slight breeze to ruffle the leaves. Nothing moved. And then something small and brown and furry scampered into the shrubs near her feet. She jumped back.

From behind, someone grabbed her arm, and she screamed.

"Dammit, Sydney, I told you to stay in the car." Luke spun her around, his eyes blazing. "You're gonna get yourself killed."

"I—I couldn't see you." Her mouth was so dry she barely got the words out. "I thought you were hurt."

His eyebrows drew together. "And? You thought you could run away."

"No." She tried to jerk her arm free from his painful grip. "I wouldn't have let you die."

He stared at her in disbelief. Confusion. A whole flood of emotions converged and then disappeared before she could decipher them. "You little fool."

"You're hurting me," she whispered.

He stared a moment longer, then blinked and dropped

his hands. His gaze went in the direction the helicopter had taken, and then he looked at her again. "Next time I tell you to stay in the car, you stay in the friggin' car."

"Screw you." She rubbed her upper arms.

He brought his attention sharply back to her. "What did you say?"

She hesitated, questioning the wisdom of angering him. But dammit, she'd actually been worried about him and he acted as if she'd committed a crime. "Screw you."

Amusement flickered in his gaze, briefly, before his expression darkened again. "Get in the car. We have to get out of here."

She looked up at the empty blue sky, the import of what just happened finally sinking in. Her stomach rolled. She pressed her lips together trying to stave off the threatening nausea. "Do you think they'll come back?"

He followed her gaze, his expression hard and frightening. "Oh, yeah." He laughed without a trace of humor. "They'll be back."

LUKE MADE SURE the Town Car was well hidden in a grove of mesquite while he procured another vehicle. He'd been tempted to boost a Chevy that would have been easy pickings and a lot easier on his wallet, but he didn't need cops on his tail. Instead, he found a small used car lot, chose a nondescript white Ford and paid cash for it.

After making a couple of calls from pay phones and replenishing their food and water, he returned to the Town Car to untie Sydney and get their bags. She'd undoubtedly be madder than a wet hen because he'd used the handcuffs, or because he'd bound and gagged her, period. But he couldn't take any chances that she'd call home.

Bad enough that he'd almost let his guard down earlier and told her more than she needed to know. But she'd surprised the hell out of him. Getting out of the car as she had, putting herself in danger because she was worried about his safety had totally blown him away. Spoiled rich girls didn't do selfless things like that. At least, not the ones he knew.

More proof that Sydney was different. Still, she was just a job, a means to pay the rent, a means to get him south of the border, and he'd damn well better keep sight of that fact. Or he could get them both killed.

He drove the Ford alongside the Town Car and parked close. Through the heavily tinted windows he saw a shadow, Sydney's head coming up. Ignoring her, he got out and opened both trunks and transferred their belongings before opening the passenger door.

Sydney glared at him. Man, he did not look forward to taking off her gag. He unlocked the handcuffs first. She didn't wait for him to remove the gag. She ripped it free herself.

"Do you know how long you've been gone?" She rubbed her reddened wrists. "I've had nothing to drink for…" She glanced at her gold Rolex. "Three hours."

He eyed the expensive watch. An easy pawn. He'd have to remember that in case he ran out of money. "There's water in there." He inclined his head toward the Ford, and her narrowed gaze followed. "Sit up front with me."

"Why are we switching cars?"

"Smart girl like you can figure it out." He checked the front and back seat of the Town Car to make sure he didn't leave anything incriminating. He straightened and saw that she hadn't moved. "If you don't want to sit up front I can tie you up in the back."

She gave him a dirty look and then climbed into the passenger side, immediately grabbing a bottle of water and downing half of it. He felt badly about letting her get so thirsty, but he'd had no choice. He couldn't have left her alone or trusted her to go with him and not start screaming bloody murder.

"Where are we going?" she asked, indelicately wiping her mouth with the back of her hand.

"East."

"Gee, I never would have figured that out."

He noticed a large darkish red mark on her knee. It was turning into one hell of a bruise. "What happened?"

She looked down, lightly touched the discolored area and winced. "I bumped it while you were playing Evel Knievel."

"Glad you have a sense of humor. You're going to need it."

"And I haven't needed it so far?"

"The sarcasm I can do without." He pulled the car out of the trees, the tires spinning in the gravel and struggling to gain purchase. After one unsuccessful attempt, he got them onto the highway. There was no traffic coming from either direction and he forced himself to relax, rolling his shoulders, trying to work out the tension.

He had no plan. Only a lot of suspicion. Worse, his gut told him he'd been screwed. He'd ignored the inner voice once before and it had cost him plenty. It had cost him everything. He wasn't going to be that stupid again.

"Pass me the water," he said, his gaze on the road.

"Not until you tell me where we're going."

He shot her a glance.

She stared back, her dark eyes mutinous, her chin lifted at a stubborn angle. "And you can tell me who those men in the helicopter were."

"I have no idea."

"Right."

"I have a suspicion," he said carefully, wanting her trust and cooperation but unwilling to reveal too much yet.

That got her interest. She narrowed her gaze. "The union?"

"Yeah." He checked the rearview mirror. Not another car in sight. Just miles of empty country highway. He hoped it stayed that way until he got a clue as to what they should do next. If things got too hairy, they could always go to Mama Sadie's place.

Damn, he didn't want to do that. Just the thought of returning to the swamps made him sweat. Made his heart pound like a mother. He'd think of something else.

"You're lying."

He grunted. "I don't know for sure. No sense in naming names."

"How honorable."

"Shit, Sydney."

"I'm merely pointing out the irony of—"

"Shut up!"

She stiffened and shrunk closer to the door. He drove another mile until the shoulder widened and then pulled the car off to the side. When he saw her reach for the door handle, he grabbed her wrist. She gasped and stared at him with frightened eyes.

"I'm not going to hurt you," he said, loosening his hold and turning off the engines.

"Why are we stopping?"

"We need to talk."

She moistened her lips, her bravado clearly faltering. God only knew what went on in that pretty head of hers, what she imagined he'd do to her.

"Okay." She settled back against the seat, angling her bruised knee toward him, her face still wary.

He released her. "This is going to be a little hard to swallow," he warned, trying to cushion his next words, amazed that he gave enough of a damn.

Curiosity flashed in her face, and then her eyes narrowed again in suspicion. "Go on."

"I didn't kidnap you," he said, and her mouth opened. "Wait. Hear me out."

She frowned and pressed her lips together. And then she seemed to relax, her expression amused and she muttered, "This ought to be good."

Smug little twit. The gloves were off. "I was hired to protect you."

Her eyebrows shot up. "Protect me?"

He nodded, watching the way her face darkened with bewilderment, the way she nibbled her lower lip.

Her chin came up with a haughtiness he hadn't seen before, defiance flashing in her eyes. "That's not possible."

Shrugging, he made a move to start the car again. "Suit yourself."

She shook her head. "By whom?"

Luke smiled. She was going to love this. "Willard Seymour."

Chapter Eight

Sydney's fingers curled into a fist. It was as if her nerve endings had ignited. "You're lying."

He held her gaze, his light blue eyes unwavering. "Why would I bother? How would I know Willard's name?"

"That wouldn't be difficult to find out."

"Again, why would I bother?"

She shook her head. At first, she'd been terrified, not knowing what Luke had in mind. Willard wouldn't have subjected her to that kind of horror. "He wouldn't do something like that. He would've told me."

"If he had, would you have allowed it?"

Staring down the vast expanse of empty highway, her mind went into overdrive. Not another car had passed them for an hour. Even if she were to get out and run, she had no place to go. No help to seek. What purpose would Luke have to lie at this point?

Still, it didn't make sense…

"You would've said he was overreacting and that you didn't need a bodyguard. Which is what you've been saying ever since you got the letters."

She swallowed. "Just because you know about the letters doesn't mean anything."

He shrugged. "How many kidnappers would provide you with Evian and imported cheese and gherkins? Think I'd be considerate enough to call your nanny for a list of your favorite foods?"

She uncapped the bottle and took another sip of water. Her mouth was so dry she wasn't sure she could speak. Not that she had a reply to his sarcasm. The bastard.

"Sydney." His voice gentled and he lightly touched her arm.

She refused to look at him. Turning her head, she stared out the window, trying to gather her thoughts. What he'd said made sense, but he'd tied her up and gagged her. Made her leave the bathroom door open. Willard would never have allowed such treatment.

"Okay," she said, facing him again. There was an easy way to settle this. "Give me your cell phone."

Slowly, he shook his head. "It needs to be charged."

"Let me see."

He withdrew it from his pocket and handed it to her. She tried Willard's number. The phone was dead. Luke took it back and slipped it into his pocket.

"What about mine? It should still be working."

"I left it back at the cabin."

"I don't believe you."

He shrugged. "I don't have it."

"And my purse?"

"Back at the cabin."

"How could you do that? I have things in there I need."

He looked her directly in the eyes. "If you recall, we left in a hurry."

She stared back, still unwilling to believe him and looking for a betraying twitch or flicker of guilt. His gaze stayed steady. If he was lying, he was damn good at it. Of course, a kidnapper had no conscience.

"Fine," she finally said. "When we get to civilization I'll use a pay phone to call Willard. In fact, I'll arrange for us to be picked up."

"I don't think so." He started the car and pulled onto the highway again.

She studied the stubborn set of his beard-roughened jaw, sure she had him cornered. He'd have no problem letting her call if he'd told the truth. "Why not?"

"It isn't safe."

"Not even a nice try."

"Look, Sydney, I shouldn't have told you. In fact, it was unethical. This isn't the first job I've done for Willard. I'm on retainer with Wainwright Corporation." He grunted. "Although it's probably my last job."

"So why did you tell me?"

His grip tightened slightly on the wheel. "Because your cooperation will make it easier to protect you."

God, she was confused. If he was lying, he was awfully damn convincing. "You're a bodyguard?"

"When necessary."

"What have you done for Wainwright Corporation?"

"Security mostly."

"We have our own security chief."

He shot her a knowing glance. "Sam Decker. Good man."

So he knew the man's name. That still didn't mean anything. "Then why would Willard keep you on retainer?"

"For internal problems. Like when Willard suspected

someone inside the company had sabotaged your Atlanta office computers."

Sydney's breath caught. There was no way Luke would know about that unless…

"It turned out to be a former employee who'd been fired for copying and selling blueprints to the competition. The guy had left a bug programmed in the mainframe in case he ever got caught. He set the chain of events in motion the day he was fired." He smiled at her. "But you already know all that, don't you, Sydney?" He returned his attention to the road. "Now you have to wonder how I know about it."

"Easy. Sam could have told you."

"Sam wasn't in on that investigation. Willard wasn't sure who was responsible. Everyone was a suspect. Even your brother Rick."

Sydney gaped at him. "Rick was never a suspect."

"Not according to Willard."

"But Willard himself—" She cut herself short. She wasn't about to discuss Rick with this criminal. Her brother had worked like a dog trying to learn the business. He'd been concerned with her welfare from the beginning, offering to move into the Wainwright estate to be with her the minute after the first threat had arrived.

"I know. Willard had him checked out. Who do you think handled the investigation?" He threw a look at the bottle of Evian she clutched so tightly it was a wonder it hadn't burst. "I'd like some of that water now."

Her heart pounded as she automatically uncapped the bottle before handing it to him. "If you had checked Rick out, then you knew he couldn't have been involved with the Atlanta office being forced to shut down."

"He was never at the top of my list but since he'd had a minor scrape with the law, Willard considered him a potential suspect."

"What do you mean scrape with the law?" This had to be another lie. Rick had checked out perfectly.

"Ah, apparently Willard doesn't tell you everything."

She gritted her teeth at his smug tone of voice, and then impatiently watched him take a long swallow of water. His throat worked with the effort and she found herself becoming mesmerized with the clean, strong line of his jaw.

"Nice." He handed her back the Evian. "Strawberry."

"What?"

"Your lip gloss."

Syd blinked, realizing that they'd just shared the bottle. She rarely got flustered, but the fact that he'd noticed the flavor sent a silly thrill down her spine that quickly turned to disgust. "The tube was in the bag you gave me. I put it on earlier to keep my lips from chapping."

"Don't get defensive. It was just a comment."

"Tell me about Rick's legal trouble."

"Nothing to tell. He'd been falsely arrested, spent three days in jail, and then was released with the Clark County's profuse apology. The end."

"But what was he arrested for?"

"It doesn't matter. He was innocent."

"It matters to me."

Luke muttered a pithy word. "What's wrong with you people? Wasn't it bad enough to have been wrongly accused, do you have to continue to crucify him?"

Momentarily taken aback by his strong reaction, she stared at him in silence. Odd. He was more than just irate, he almost seemed to be defending Rick.

"Look," she said finally. "I love my brother. I was thrilled he came into my life. But you said yourself that we're in a dangerous situation, and if there's anything I should know about—"

"There isn't. You'll have to trust me on that."

She laughed humorlessly at the irony. "For someone who's taken me against my will, you've been asking for a hell of a lot of trust."

"You're right." He turned those cool blue eyes on her. "What's the alternative?"

AFTER AN HOUR of emotionally charged silence, Sydney fell asleep. Luke looked over at her. Her head was tilted to the side, her mouth slightly parted. She looked young. Younger than twenty-five. Yet she was about to be handed the reins of a multimillion-dollar company. He sure as hell didn't envy her the responsibility.

Or the money. He didn't envy that either. That kind of wealth brought trouble. Man, did he know about that, and he hadn't even had the pleasure of spending the dough. Not that he could've bought much in prison.

The thought of that hellhole where he'd wasted a year of his life brought on the usual fury. He had to tamp it down. His energy was better used toward figuring out their next move. Bad enough she had him second-guessing himself. Had he missed something in Rick's past that might make him a threat? Had Luke's scorn for the failings of the justice system blinded him? Just because Rick had been innocent of a juvenile crime didn't absolve him now.

Luke blinked a couple of times, trying to keep himself from becoming mesmerized by the road. He needed sleep. Even for just a few hours. They'd stop soon and find a motel, probably within a half hour. A mile back, he'd seen a sign for Hartsville. If it were like most small towns in this part of Texas, there'd be a motel, a gas station and a market. Everything they needed. And there'd be a pay phone. The first thing Sydney would want to do was call Willard.

Luke stretched his neck to the side, loosening the tension that knotted the muscles all the way down to his shoulders. Hell, maybe he ought to let her call. See who showed up after that. At least he'd know what and whom he was dealing with. Then maybe he'd decide to let the police in on what was happening.

Or he could just walk away. Turn Sydney loose. She was a big girl. He could lay out his suspicions, let her interpret them as she wished. Then she could take care of herself and decide what she wanted to do.

He almost missed the turnoff for Hartsville and had to take a sharp turn. Sydney stirred but didn't open her eyes. She made a soft mewing sound that got to him more than it should have.

Shit, he knew damn well he couldn't leave her to her own devices. She was a sitting duck and she was too naive to understand the danger. Too sheltered and trusting to believe that someone close to her, someone she cared about, wanted her dead.

"WHERE ARE we?" Sydney blinked. It seemed like they'd just gotten on the road and here they were sitting in a motel parking lot.

She wrinkled her nose. A horrid-looking motel, at that. Peeling paint, holes in the screens, faded green doors and a roof that didn't look as if it could withstand the next thunderstorm.

"Hartsville."

"We're still in Texas, right?"

"Yep. We'll stay here for the night."

The sun hadn't set yet. She looked at her watch. Only six-fifteen. She had no intention of spending the night here in this godforsaken place. As soon as she contacted Willard, he'd send someone for her. "Have you seen a pay phone?"

"Nope."

"Would you tell me if you had?"

He smiled. "You could probably use the office phone if you call collect."

"You don't have a problem with me calling Willard?"

"Nope."

She didn't get it. This was too easy. She'd expected him to discourage her from calling. What the hell was he up to? Lulling her into a false sense of security? It didn't matter. She wasn't going to miss this opportunity.

Before she opened her door, she looked around the parking lot and down the narrow road that led back toward the highway. There weren't any other cars in sight except for a white rusted truck parked at the small diner across the street. On the corner was a two-pump gas station that looked as if it had been abandoned.

"We weren't followed." Luke glanced in the rearview mirror, his expression grim. "It's safe. I've already checked the place out."

Odd that she believed him, or that she had to rely on him. But she did. She got out of the car, her leg muscles aching from sitting too long, her neck stiff. She stretched it from side to side.

Maybe Luke was telling the truth. Maybe that's why he'd changed his mind about her calling Willard, because he was tired of risking his neck for her. So who were those guys who'd been chasing them?

Pressing two fingers to her temple, she took a deep breath, hoping the fuzziness would leave her brain. She didn't know what to think anymore. She had to call Willard, that's all. Confirm Luke's story.

She eyed him as he unhurriedly got out of the car and went around to the trunk and opened it. He sure didn't act like a man with anything to hide.

She checked her reflection in the side mirror. Her hair was a mess, tangled and dull looking. Hard to believe it had been perfectly styled two days ago. The thought reminded her of Julie. And then of Jeff. Her chest tightened. She didn't care so much about Jeff. But she and Julie had been good friends once.

Humiliation lingered but it occurred to her that she should tell Luke that the woman who answered Jeff's phone was Julie, and how the two should have no connection.

Out of the corner of her eye, she saw Luke watching her and she straightened. "Why did you change your mind about me calling Willard?"

"I was hired to protect you. The situation has changed. I'm not sure I can do that anymore."

She nodded. "I don't blame you for quitting."

He slid her an odd look, kind of resentful, but said nothing.

She hadn't meant to offend him if that's what she'd

done. Her comment had been sincere but she decided to leave it alone and just watched him unload their bags and the cooler. She thought briefly about stopping him. They wouldn't be staying here. At least, she wouldn't. As soon as she spoke to Willard, he'd send someone for her and this nightmare would all be over.

In fact, he'd come himself. On the company plane. He had to be frantic over her disappearance. Rick, too. No matter what Luke had implied, she trusted her brother. Willard trusted him.

She turned toward the office and got only a few feet when Luke said, "He's not there."

"Who?"

"There's a sign on the door saying they'd be back in half an hour."

"But how can I—" She bit back a pithy remark when she realized he had no intention of letting her call.

He looked at his watch, a ghost of a smile lurking at the corners of his mouth. "Which is now in ten minutes."

Bastard. He could toy with her all he wanted. When Willard showed up, Luke wouldn't be so smug. She'd see that he got paid what he was promised. But he'd never work for Wainwright Corporation again.

She folded her arms across her chest and took a step back to avoid a huge crack in the sidewalk. "I don't like it here."

"Tough." He got out a bag of groceries.

It took all her willpower to hold on to her temper. "Assuming you've told me the truth, you're actually in my employ, correct?"

A mocking smile lifted his lips and he slowly nodded.

"Then I call the shots."

His eyebrows drew together in a brief frown, and then the smile was back, a slight curve of his mouth. Just enough to annoy her. "Whatever you say, boss." He looked past her. "He's back."

She spun around in time to see a short, paunchy man pull the sign off the door and enter the office. He waved to them and then stood at the open door, mopping his forehead with a red handkerchief as she hurried toward him.

"You folks checking in?" he asked around a toothpick dangling from the corner of his mouth.

"Yes," she said, cringing at the lie and promising herself she'd reward him later when Willard got here. She smiled. "But I'd like to use your phone, if it's all right."

His bushy, graying eyebrows drew together. "Long distance?"

"I'm calling collect."

His gaze strayed past her toward Luke, and then he motioned her inside. "Come on in."

She waited while he got the operator and then summoned her patience when he hovered over her while she gave the woman Willard's private number. Although she figured he'd still be at the office, she'd have preferred calling his cell phone, but then she couldn't have called collect.

It rang twice, and it was Rick who answered and accepted the charges in a hoarse, anxious voice when the operator identified Syd as the caller.

As good as it was to hear his voice, she hesitated, wanting to talk to Willard, hating the fear that spawned doubt and suspicion. Fear that Luke had planted in her mind. She loathed that she suddenly didn't have the faith in Rick that she should have. Even after he'd proven himself over and over again.

"Sydney, is that you?" He sounded frightened, angry, disbelieving.

"Rick?"

"Sydney?" His voice was reed thin and then hesitated again. "Christ, Sydney, is that you?"

"Yes." She swallowed back the sudden lump threatening to block her vocal cords.

"Where are you?"

"Where's Willard?"

"Are you okay?"

"I'm fine. Really. Where's Willard?" She heard the office door creak open and glanced over her shoulder. Luke had come inside and nodded to the clerk who'd reclaimed his seat behind the metal office desk. He'd turned on a small television and barely paid them any attention.

"Down the hall. Where the hell are you?"

Again, she hesitated. If only Willard would get back...

"Dammit, Syd. We haven't heard anything since the ransom demand."

"What ransom?" Her eyes met Luke's, his narrowing slightly.

"They insisted on no police and said they'd call back, but nothing. You're sure you're okay?"

Across the line, she heard a noise in the background and then Willard's voice.

"It's Sydney," Rick said.

"Sydney!" Willard was on the line. "Good God, child, where are you?"

"Hi, Willard," she said in a small voice, horrified that she had to blink back tears. He sounded worried enough. And then there was Luke watching...

Her gaze briefly met his before she turned away and furtively dabbed at her eyes.

"Where are you?" Willard asked again.

"A town called Hartsville. I'm with Luke." She paused, waiting for Willard to either express his relief or question Luke's identity.

Before he could do either, Luke grabbed the phone. She tried to snatch it back, certain he was about to hang up, but he put the receiver to his ear.

"Mr. Seymour, we have a situation."

"Give me the damn phone." Sydney tried to get it back, but Luke was tall enough to keep it out of her reach.

The man at the desk ignored them and just kept his attention on *Wheel of Fortune* playing on the small TV.

"I managed to lose them but I figure they'll still be looking." He paused. "Southeast of Dallas," Luke said. "About six hours by car." He looked at the clerk. "Anywhere to land a small plane around here?"

The guy frowned at Luke as if he had sprouted a second head.

"I haven't finished speaking to Willard." Sydney got right in Luke's face. "Give me the phone now."

"Dew Drop Inn. It's the only motel in town." He stared down at her. "We'll be here waiting."

She glared back and held out her hand.

Luke replaced the receiver on the cradle, severing the connection.

Syd stared at the phone, and then transferred her furious gaze to Luke. "You stupid bastard."

The clerk looked up then, and cleared his throat. "You folks wanna check in now?"

Without breaking eye contact with her, Luke laid down cash on the desk. "This enough for one night?"

The guy grabbed the bills and flipped through them. "Yeah, that'll take care of it." He stuffed the money in his pocket. "We got something for you to fill out. Me, I don't care what you call yourselves. Sign Smith if you want." Grinning, he laid a key numbered *Six* on the desk and then went back to watching *Wheel of Fortune*.

Sydney reached for the phone.

Luke caught her by the wrist. "No need to do that, darlin'," he said, his face dark and challenging. "You'll be seeing Willard in a couple of hours."

"I want to talk to him now."

"You got what you wanted. Come on." He motioned toward the door.

"Got what I wanted?" She shook her head in disbelief. He hadn't given her time to confirm his far-fetched claim. "I only heard your side of the conversation. For all I know, you could have been setting up a ransom drop."

He muttered a curse, tightened his hold on her wrist and pulled her toward the door, but she was ready to make a scene if she had to. Twisting her hand, she tried to break free, but he caught her around the waist, pulled her against him and kissed her. A hard, punishing kiss that stole her breath and shocked her speechless.

His beard-roughened chin scraped her face and she shoved at his chest until he finally withdrew. A slow grin lifted the corners of his mouth, his gaze lingering on her suddenly parched lips. He winked at the clerk, who watched them with new interest.

"Looks like I got myself a prickly bride," Luke said, and picked her up, threw her over his shoulder and carried her out of the office.

Chapter Nine

Sydney moved the faded plaid chair by the window, sat down on the lumpy seat and stared outside. If she never saw Luke again after today, it would be too soon. He'd been high-handed, unnecessarily rough and, in general, a barbarian. She had a good mind to tell Willard not to pay him. Assuming Willard had really hired him.

How could she be sure? Why had he grabbed the phone from her? Because he'd made the ransom demand? That was the only thing that made sense. Which meant he didn't expect Willard to come and get her. Luke expected Willard to bring money. Then would he let her go?

She turned her head slightly and caught a glimpse of him in the mirror over the dresser. He was doing something to his watch, his brows furrowed in thought.

What worried her the most was that she didn't want to believe that Luke was a criminal, that he was willing to exchange her for money. She wanted to believe that he was her bodyguard. But blind faith would be foolish. She needed to keep up her guard.

And dammit, she needed to forget that kiss. Not that he'd meant anything by it other than to distract her and the clerk, but that didn't stop her from remembering the warm softness of his lips, the way her heart had pounded against his strong solid chest.

She looked up and caught him watching her.

"Why can't I have my own room?" she asked. "Is it too much to want a little privacy?"

He eyed her with one of those amused looks that grated on her nerves. "What if those guys show up again? What would you do? Scream?"

"Give me my gun back and I'll show you."

He smiled. "You didn't know how to use it the first time."

She turned back to the window. The diner had already closed. Only one car had passed in the last half hour. Didn't anyone live here?

"Are you hungry?" He moved closer to her, and she clenched her teeth at the ridiculous way her body reacted to his nearness.

She carefully avoided looking at him. "Too late. The diner's closed."

"We have fruit and cheese in the cooler."

"No thanks."

"You'd better eat something."

"I'll wait until Willard gets here."

"Why? Does he have to spoon feed you?"

"Go to hell."

"No thanks, darlin', I've already been there." He pulled his shirt up, exposing a taut muscular belly.

Her breath caught. Her chest tightened. What was he doing taking his clothes off?

He took the gun out of the waistband of his jeans and then let the shirt fall back into place.

She moistened her lips, ashamed at her disappointment. How could she be feeling this attraction? He could be lying, for all she knew. Simply waiting to get money out of Willard. Still, her heart overruled and blocked her mind from believing such a vile thought.

After all, he hadn't been unkind to her. And he had protected her from those men. Granted, she didn't know much about him, but he treated her well enough, considering.

She watched him pace to the other window and wondered what he'd meant about already having been to hell. In fact, she was beginning to wonder a lot about Luke. Maybe later, when this was over, he'd tell her about himself.

He idly glanced outside, then pointed the gun at the ceiling and checked the chamber, bringing her back to reality. They weren't friends. There wasn't going to be a later for them. Once Willard came for her, she'd never see Luke again. "What's that for?"

He tucked the gun back into his waistband. "Just checking it out."

A sudden thought knotted her stomach. "You aren't going to shoot Willard."

"Not unless he shoots first," he said, and then gave her one of those annoying smiles of his.

"This isn't funny." She drew her knees up to her chest and wrapped her arms around them, hugging them tightly. Oddly, she was more frightened now than before she knew Willard was coming for her. If he hurt Willard in any way...

Luke seemed to sober quickly. "I'm just being cautious. That's all."

Her gaze searched the room, hoping she'd see a

phone she'd missed the first time. She couldn't bear it if anything happened to Willard. It would be like losing her parents all over again.

God, she swore she'd never be flip with him again. If he wanted her to start taking limos, she'd do it. No more arguments. No more asserting her independence at the cost of his peace of mind. "If you'd just let me talk to Willard again, I'd feel so much better."

Luke shook his head, went to the cooler and got out a bottle of water and two apples. When he tried to hand her the water and one of the apples, she refused them. That didn't stop him from chomping into the dark red fruit and then tipping his head back and taking a long drink of the Evian.

She tried not to watch the way his throat worked, or notice how he pursed his lips around the tip of the bottle. He had a great mouth, she'd give him that. His eyes weren't too bad either, the lightness a nice contrast to his dark hair. Under any other circumstance he might seem attractive.

"Change your mind?" He held up the bottle, one side of his mouth lifting in that insolent smile she despised.

Realizing that she'd been staring, she turned away. "Don't you ever shave?"

"Occasionally. Why?" The laughter in his voice fueled her irritation. "You plan on kissing me again?"

"In your dreams." She turned back to him, her gaze narrowed and purposeful. "Furthermore, I didn't kiss you. And if you ever do anything like that again, the only thing else you'll be kissing is your paycheck goodbye."

He chuckled and checked his watch, his obvious lack of concern heightening her annoyance. She'd never met anyone like him before. Nor did anyone get under her skin like he did. The thought gave her pause. It wasn't as if she was spoiled or a snob or anything, but she wasn't accustomed to being dismissed.

"Last chance if you want an apple," he said, and then put it back in the cooler when she snubbed him. "If you want to grab a shower, I suggest you do it now."

She slid a glance toward the bathroom and the ugly yellow linoleum. "I'll wait."

"I wouldn't."

She stared at him in disbelief, resisting the urge to sniff herself. "What are you implying?"

He met her eyes. He seemed hesitant. "That you may not have another chance for a while."

"Willard is flying, isn't he?"

"I believe so."

"Then I'll be home in a matter of hours."

The pitying look he gave her made her uneasy. So brief she could easily have imagined it, but she didn't think she had. He'd been acting a bit odd ever since they'd stopped at the motel.

She watched him stow the cooler near the door with their two bags and it occurred to her that he hadn't ordered her to unpack. Obviously he didn't expect them to be staying. A good sign that he expected her to leave with Willard. She wondered where Luke was headed. Back to Dallas with them?

The thought held more appeal than it should, even if only long enough for him to collect his pay, and she forced her attention off the breadth of his shoulders, the snug fit of his jeans. Darkness had gathered and with the diner closed and no other rooms rented, the only light was from two streetlamps and a soft glow from the office.

She slouched down in the chair until she got comfortable and daydreamed about the hot tub in her bathroom, imagining the streams of water jetting out to soothe her aching muscles after being handcuffed, tied up and having fallen asleep in the most awkward places.

How much had she taken her comfortable life for granted? Absent from worries of layoffs or rent increases or rising gas prices, had she ever stopped to appreciate the security she enjoyed? Or sympathized with those who lived from one paycheck to the next, or worse, didn't have a bed to sleep in each night.

The past twenty-four hours had given her a lot to think about. Ironically, her experience had strengthened her resolve to divide the company rather than back off as the union wanted. Why shouldn't the men and women who'd made the company a giant enjoy the spoils?

She let her thoughts wander aimlessly until she started to doze, but caught herself when her head started to droop. She brought it up sharply and looked at Luke. He sat at the edge of the bed, his long legs spread and stretched out in front of him while he stared at his watch and rubbed the back of his neck.

He looked tired, too. Lines of tension had formed around his mouth, and the skin was a little dark under his eyes. Made them look all the bluer.

She checked her own watch and realized with a start that she had actually dozed off because a phantom hour had passed. "How much longer do you think it'll be?" she asked, and he looked up, his gaze alert before that pitying look entered his eyes again.

Slowly, he got to his feet and went to his bag and got something out she couldn't see. Even when he approached her she couldn't see what he had fisted in his hand. He got so close that she reared her head back. He reached for her and her heart nearly exploded.

She held her breath.

Oh, God… He was going to kiss her again…

"Sorry about this, Sydney," he said quietly, and pulled her to her feet.

She started to scream when she saw the familiar red scarf. But he covered her mouth with one hand while he fastened the silk around her wrists.

PARKED IN the shadows, Luke glanced over the backseat at Sydney. He couldn't see her face. Just as well. He only needed to know she wasn't going anywhere or able to warn Willard. Or whoever showed up. His money was still on Willard. But he couldn't discount the brother. Rick had a lot to gain by getting rid of Sydney. Like a hundred million bucks.

Then again, it could be anyone close to Willard and Sydney who'd showed up at the cabin, or thugs from the union. Someone he hadn't considered because Luke had no reason to look for motive. The job was supposed to have been simple. Keep Sydney safe and out of the way until the legal eagles transferred the company.

Using him was a pretty tidy plan. Kill them both and then accuse him of kidnapping after the fact. A bitter ex-con looking for a quick score. Hell, who wouldn't buy it?

He craned his neck to look down the highway. He wouldn't be able to see a car but he'd see headlights. The town couldn't have been more perfect. Small, deserted, in the middle of nowhere. If fireworks went off, there wouldn't be any bystanders to get caught in the crossfire.

Not much light came from the office. No lamp, just the flickering glow of the television. Hopefully, the clerk was sound asleep by now. There'd be no need for anyone to bother with him, except maybe to ask when Luke and Sydney had checked out. Of course, the guy knew nothing. He'd be as surprised as anyone that his customers had disappeared.

A light still burned in the room Luke had rented. He'd purposely left it on as a beacon. According to the clerk, someone had called to make sure he and Sydney were registered there. Now all they could do was wait.

Sydney moaned, probably trying to get his attention. He took the bait and turned to look at her. She'd managed to pull herself to a sitting position and was making furious expressions as she tried unsuccessfully to jerk free.

"What?" he asked. "Thirsty?"

She started to give an angry shake of her head, then reconsidered and nodded.

Yeah, right. She was so transparent he wanted to laugh. If he were to take the gag off for a second she'd be screaming her head off. "You can hold on for another half hour."

She made a frustrated guttural sound in her throat.

He didn't blame her for being upset. She didn't understand and he couldn't explain that this was for her own safety. Even if he did explain, she wouldn't believe him. If his estimate was right, very soon she'd see for herself why this was necessary.

Damn if he didn't feel bad for her. For the painful

dose of reality she was about to experience. Of course, he could be wrong, and he hoped he was. For both their sakes.

He thought he saw a flicker of light coming from around the bend of the highway. Hard to see for sure, parked far back in the trees as they were, but it was the perfect spot to see the motel yet stay hidden.

A moment later, headlights appeared and he braced himself for what might come. Sure enough, the late-model black car slowed as it approached the motel, stopped for a few seconds and then turned into the parking lot. The windows were heavily tinted, concealing the occupants. The license plates were from Texas but so covered with mud you couldn't make out the numbers. Deliberately, no doubt.

A tall slim man wearing a black Stetson got out of the passenger side and just stood there, looking around. The driver stayed put. No telling if anyone else was in the backseat.

Only one other car, probably belonging to the clerk, was parked in the lot close to the office. The guy in the Stetson headed straight for their room.

Obviously having spotted the car herself, Sydney started straining against the gag, trying to talk, moving her body excitedly.

"Do you recognize that guy?" Luke asked her.

She ignored him, bucking and jerking, trying to free herself.

Luke cupped his hand behind her nape and forced her to look at the man and the car. "This is important, Sydney. Concentrate. Do you recognize the man or the car?"

She stilled and narrowed her gaze. After a moment, she slowly shook her head.

"Take your time," Luke said. "I know it's far and the lighting is poor, but is there anything familiar at all about him, like the hat or the way he walks?"

She made a sound of frustration and shook her head again.

He released her, his gaze fastened on the man knocking on the door of room number six. That she didn't recognize him meant nothing. More likely the guy was a hired thug. But if they could link him to Willard...

The man looked around, and seeing no one, kicked in the door and then entered the room.

Sydney gasped. She stared as the driver got out. Shorter and stockier than his colleague, he followed him inside, keeping his arm close to his side, as if he might be shielding a rifle.

"What about him?" Luke asked her. "Know who he is?"

Again, she shook her head, her confused, frightened eyes meeting his. He looked away, and saw the driver come back outside and walk toward the office.

He hoped the other guy was piecing together the bogus clues Luke had left behind. A torn map had been dropped in the wastebasket, the missing section indicating interest in a southern route. Scribbling on a crumbled slip of paper would further lead the men on a wild goose chase to El Paso.

Before the driver got to the office, the door opened and the clerk stepped outside. They talked for a moment, the clerk shrugging, scratching his balding head, obviously equally mystified over the disappearance of his customers.

The guy in the Stetson came out of the room and the clerk straightened. He looked around the shorter, stockier man and then hurried toward room six, gesturing and shouting. The splintered door barely hung on to the hinges.

After more shouting, the clerk ran toward the office. He didn't have a chance. Luke saw the flash of the gun barrel a second before the driver raised his arm, took aim and fired.

The shot echoed off the building as the man crumpled to the asphalt. Luke immediately looked at Sydney. Her wide-eyed stare didn't waver, an eerie sound coming from deep in her throat, and then she jerked and seemed to be having trouble catching her breath.

Without hesitation he removed the gag. "Take it easy," he said gently, rubbing the back of her neck. "You don't want to start hyperventilating."

"Oh, my God—"

His hand firmed on her nape for emphasis. "Keep it down, Sydney."

"But did you see—" She hiccupped, fought for a breath. "We have to go help that man."

"It's too late."

"You don't know that." She kept shaking her head. "They shot him. My God—they just shot him." Tinged with hysteria, her voice started to rise again.

"Sydney, listen." He darted a look toward the motel. The men were getting in their car. "Pull yourself together. Don't make me gag you again."

"But that man from the motel. He could still be alive…"

"No, Sydney." Luke touched her cheek. He knew

better. The shooter was a pro. He'd shot the clerk in the head. The poor old man wouldn't be around to tell any tales. "He's already dead."

"You can't know that," she said in a small voice, her gaze inexorably glued to the scene.

"Yeah, I do." He didn't want to be cruel and point out the obvious. Half the guy's brains had spilled out and pooled around him. He hadn't expected that to happen. "I think you do, too."

She briefly glanced at Luke, the shock making her face a pasty white, and then stared in silence as the black car pulled out of the parking lot, slowly cruising toward the opposite end of town.

"Who—" Her voice caught on a sob. "Who were those men?"

"I don't know." He waited until the car was out of sight and then studied her face, mentally debating how much to tell her. Now wasn't the time, he decided. It was enough of a blow for her to finally realize that she really was a target. "Turn around. I'll untie you."

As if she hadn't heard him, she stayed perfectly still, staring straight ahead.

"Sydney?"

She looked at him, and then slowly turned so that he could reach her bound wrists. He unknotted the scarf and pulled it free. She crumpled into a heap against the door, hugging her drawn knees, resting her forehead on them so that he couldn't see her face. "What are we going to do now?" she asked in a quiet, muffled voice.

"Stay put for a while. Make sure they've left the area. They should be heading southwest if they picked up on the clues I dropped."

Her chin slowly came up and she stared at him. "You knew this was going to happen. You let an innocent man die."

"Don't be stupid. I didn't think it would play out like this."

"You knew. You set this whole thing up."

He cursed. "I was only trying to flush out whoever is after you."

"Oh, God." She closed her eyes and tapped her head back against the window a couple of times. "That poor man died because of me."

"Trying to assign blame isn't going to help a damn thing. Besides, this isn't just about you anymore, Sydney," he said, surprised and moved that she wasn't thinking only about herself. "Someone's trying to frame me for this mess."

"How?"

"I'm supposed to have kidnapped you, remember? You die, and then I get killed while someone is trying to *save* you, and the case is solved in one neat little package."

She straightened, shaking her head. "But Willard would explain that he hired you."

Luke said nothing, waiting for her to arrive at the same conclusion he had…that Willard could very well be the person responsible.

"No." She stared at him, her eyes widening. "You're wrong. My God, how could you even think something like that?"

"You tell me, Sydney."

"What do you mean?"

"Why would Willard want you dead?"

"You bastard. He loves me. He's been like a father to me." Like a child, she flattened a hand over each ear. "I won't listen to you."

Luke dragged his gaze away from her pale, frightened face and focused on the highway, waiting for her to pull herself together. She'd just been through a major trauma. Witnessing a murder was bad enough, but trying to assume the responsibility for it was pretty staggering.

That she'd been willing to risk her life to help the clerk had blown Luke away. Probably just an impulsive response but most women he knew would have wanted to crawl into a little ball until the unpleasantness passed, especially ones of Sydney's social class. Actually, he wasn't sure he knew anyone that rich.

He kept his eyes trained on the road, although he didn't expect to see the dark late-model sedan return. He sure as hell hoped they were headed in the wrong direction, burning rubber, intending to catch up with their targets.

Luke checked his watch. Only three minutes had passed. It felt like an hour. Even though the town was deserted at this hour, someone could have heard the shot and Luke had no intention of being anywhere in the vicinity if the highway patrol showed up. Fortunately for him, way out here that was liable to take a while, too.

A noise came from the backseat. He looked over his shoulder. Sydney sat with her hands covering her face, her shoulders shaking as she tried to control the sobs. "Sydney?"

She wouldn't answer. Just turned away.

"Sydney."

"What?" she muttered curtly.

Now that he had her attention, he had no idea what to say. "Don't cry."

"I'm not." She buried her face deeper, drew her knees up closer to her body.

He went back to watching the road, cursing under his breath. What the hell was he supposed to do now?

Another soft sob finally undid him. He rubbed his eyes, cast a final look toward the deserted highway and then swung a leg over the seat. Climbing over was awkward at his height but he finally managed to maneuver his body over the seat and landed next to Sydney.

She started, and for a moment he thought she was going to bolt. But she sniffed loudly, then wiped her eyes and stared at him with resentment.

"What about the ransom demand?" she asked. "That proves it can't be Willard."

The hair on the back of Luke's neck stood. "What ransom demand?"

"The one Willard got."

"He told you that?"

She thought for a minute. "No, Rick did."

What was happening? There was no demand. Either Rick or Willard could've been lying. But which one?

"You're wrong about Willard," she said in a weak voice that broke on a sob.

"You're right," he said, moving closer and sliding his arm around her shoulders.

"You are." She covered her face, obviously trying not to cry or at least not let him see her cry.

He tightened his arm around her, pulled her against his chest, and let her cry.

Chapter Ten

"What do you think?" Luke asked as he pulled in front of the Lazy River Motel sign.

The pink adobe building was on the outskirts of a small town still quiet during the dawn hours. Sydney had to admit it looked better than most of the ones they'd passed. It even boasted a pool and hot tub.

She shrugged. "Fine."

"We can keep going if you want."

Rubbing her weary eyes, she shook her head. She hadn't even been driving and she was bone-tired. She couldn't imagine how exhausted Luke was, yet he was willing to drive on to accommodate her. He'd been really great. Made her want to start crying all over again.

"I'll go check us in," he said, turning off the ignition and then stretching out his back and shoulders. "Two rooms, I presume?"

She swallowed and murmured, "One is fine."

He hesitated but she refused to look at him; instead, she rummaged through the bag of toiletries until he finally got out of the car. She hoped he didn't get the wrong idea, that she was softening toward him after his unexpected display of kindness. She felt safer sharing a room. That's all.

She watched as he paused to stretch again, his arms over his head, his T-shirt riding up and exposing his narrow waist. The memory of that night in the cabin, of him running naked out of the bathroom rushed through her. Heat spread throughout her chest and up her neck.

At the time, she'd been scared to death, afraid he'd rape her or worse. That seemed like a century ago. Now, she vividly recalled the slimness of his hips, the width of his shoulders, the tan line that ended low on his hips, how firm and taut his entire body was, as if he worked at it every day. Although she doubted he'd waste his time that way.

He had strong arms, too, that could restrain her without effort, but that had also cradled her with a gentleness that made her weep. Made her want to believe every word he said, even when it was too painful to hear.

God, but he confused her. One minute she wanted to run as far away from him as she could, and the next, she wanted to crawl into his lap and let him kiss her hair, rub the side of her arms just as he had earlier.

After that man was murdered.

She bit her lip. She couldn't go there. Couldn't think about that right now. The trembling started inside again. Bile rose in her throat.

She closed her eyes and forced herself to think about the trip she'd made to the Alps last summer. The train ride she'd taken to Interlaken had been spectacular. Much colder than she'd expected, but well worth the trip.

The small mountain community was like a fairy tale come to life and she'd been fortunate enough to see a wedding unfold. The bride rode to the church in a horse-drawn carriage streaming with wild flowers. Sydney had decided then that was how she wanted to get married.

If she lived long enough.

She shivered and opened her eyes.

Luke stood outside watching her. He opened the driver's door and got in without a word.

"We're not staying?"

"There's a room in the back." He reversed the car and headed around the building. "By the way, we're the Masters from Oklahoma and we have a baby with us."

She frowned. "You said you sent those men in the other direction."

"Just a precaution. If they do any checking, a couple with a baby might throw them off."

She waited until he parked in front of the last unit at the far end of the second building where there were no other cars. "Maybe I should try calling Willard again."

"No."

"I'll call from your cell. No one will know where I'm calling from."

"What purpose would that serve?"

She hesitated. "I don't know."

He snorted. "You plan on telling him where we are again?"

"I don't know," she ground out, angry and confused.

Luke turned off the engine and stared at her. "Don't you get it yet?"

"You don't know that it's Willard."

"Grow up, Sydney."

"If you knew, you'd have called the police. But you haven't because you don't have any proof." The simple logic reassured her. "It could be Rick or Jeff. Or maybe Julie and Jeff are in it together. Or maybe it really is the union. They could've had Willard's phone tapped or something."

"Who's Julie?"

"My hairdresser."

"And?"

"She's also an old friend from prep school."

"Jeff's the guy you've been seeing, right?" He frowned. "What's your point?"

Humiliation gripped her. She'd always been careful with men, keeping a distance until she felt reasonably sure it didn't matter to them that she was a Wainwright. Obviously, she'd been foolish for letting Jeff into her life.

She opened the car door. "I have to go to the bathroom."

Thankfully, Luke said nothing. Just got out and opened the motel room door. She didn't help carry in anything but the bag of toiletries that was on her lap, then headed straight for the bathroom.

She closed and locked the door, lowered the toilet seat cover and sat. Unfortunately, the mirror was low enough that she could see herself. What a mess. Her hair spiked out in several directions, red swollen eyes, smudged face, like something out of a B movie. She barely recognized herself. She could walk into the Wainwright offices right now and no one would know who she was.

She sniffed, grabbed some toilet paper and wiped her nose. Maybe that's what she ought to do. Disappear. Change her name. Get a job in some small town. Who'd truly miss her besides Willard and Rick?

Assuming they didn't want her dead.

A small moan escaped her and she covered her mouth. That she could even have such a thought angered her. Damn Luke. He'd poisoned her mind. She didn't know him. Why should she believe anything he said?

"Sydney?" He knocked at the door. "You okay?"

"Fine." She got up, grabbed more of the too-rough toilet paper and dabbed at her nose and eyes, threw the paper in the toilet and flushed it.

He stood near one of the twin beds unloading a bag when she walked out, his gaze staying on her as she paced to the window. Outside was nothing but parking lot.

"Tell me about this Julie," he said without preamble.

Keeping her attention focused outside, Syd sighed. She had to tell him. She should have already done so. "The other day when I phoned Jeff and a woman answered…" She took a breath, loath to explain yet knowing it was important. "It was Julie."

"And?" One simple word, yet its quiet austerity had the power to make her want to crawl inside herself.

"I didn't think they knew each other."

He muttered a pithy four-letter word. "You didn't think that was important enough to tell me?"

"Not at the time."

"What else?"

She turned to face him. His grim expression made her regret the petty pride that made her withhold the information. "What do you mean?"

"Why shouldn't they know each other?"

"There'd be no reason. They travel in different social circles."

"You said she went to prep school with you."

Syd moved away from the window and sat on one of

the two high-back wooden chairs flanking a small table. "It's a long story."

Luke snorted. "Sweetheart, we have nothing but time."

"It's irrelevant."

"I'll be the judge of that."

She looked into his implacable face. "Julie's mother was a waitress at a diner who married money when Julie was fourteen. Her stepfather sent her to Andrews Academy where I attended school. We became friends."

"I'm still not following. Wouldn't that place her in the same social circle?"

She shook her head. "Her mom and stepfather later divorced and things changed for Julie."

Something that looked like disgust flickered in his eyes. "She was ostracized."

She struggled to hold on to her temper. The self-righteous expression on his face made her want to slap him. "Not exactly."

"You're holding something back."

"I don't feel comfortable talking about Julie. She may not be guilty of anything and it isn't right to discuss her."

"She's guilty of banging your boyfriend, isn't she?"

Syd glared at him, keeping her fists clenched so she didn't give in to the urge to slap the smug look off his face. "He wasn't my boyfriend, number one, and secondly, that isn't what this conversation is about, is it? Or are you purposely trying to humiliate me?"

He reared his head back, looking surprised, and then his eyes narrowed with impatience. "I'm only trying to find out what the hell the connection is between those two."

"That's the problem. I don't know."

"Then give me the damn pieces of the puzzle and let me figure it out."

Suddenly, he crossed the room toward her; fearful, she was ready to jump from her chair when he stopped and jerked out the one across from her and sat down.

She breathed easier, but she couldn't relax. She hated this. Julie was a private person who abhorred gossip more than anything. God knew, she'd already been the center of enough petty speculation.

"If you and your friends suddenly ditched her after the divorce, that could make her pretty bitter, maybe want to get even," Luke said and watched Sydney's eyes widen with indignation and hurt.

"I never shunned her," she said, shaking her head. "I wouldn't do that. Julie was the one who wouldn't return my phone calls. And then she and her mother moved away and we lost all contact."

"Why did she suddenly withdraw like that?"

"She was embarrassed."

"How did the rest of your friends treat her?"

Sydney looked down and stared at her hands. "The other girls never really accepted her. They only invited her to parties when I twisted their arms. It wasn't right, but I could only do so much to include her."

Luke studied her with interest. So many facets to Sydney Wainwright. Loyal to a fault. Generous. Democratic. Socially responsible. Someone had raised her well. He doubted it was her father. Luke knew too much about him and his ruthless business dealings.

"I had the feeling she believed the divorce was her fault but she wouldn't discuss it," she continued. "I suspected she'd been abused by her stepfather." She looked up and shrugged. "That was later, when I got older, but I guess that has nothing to do with anything."

"Maybe not. But I prefer you don't leave anything out." This was hard for her, he realized. Not because she wanted to hide anything, but she genuinely disliked delving into anyone's personal life. "When was the next time you saw Julie?"

"About four months ago."

"Where?"

"At the salon where I go."

He snorted with disbelief. "You didn't think that was a coincidence?"

"Sure. I even mentioned it to her. She told me she'd gotten her cosmetology license a couple of years ago and had been working in smaller spas not making much money. When the opportunity to work at Divas came up she jumped at the chance. The tips alone are probably more than she was making giving perms and haircuts."

"I take it Divas is some swanky overpriced salon."

Annoyance flashed in her eyes. "They offer a variety of services."

"Don't get your panties in a twist. I wasn't making social commentary."

"I won't apologize to you for being rich."

"My point is, a job at a place like that couldn't be easy to come by."

"I guess not."

"You didn't use your influence to help her?"

"No." Clearly agitated, she pushed her hair back. "I was as surprised as anyone to see her." She met his eyes, her gaze wary and probing. "She'd just done my hair before you picked me up. She was the one who had a car service called for me. And you showed up."

He ignored her subtle accusation, expecting her to have waves of doubt. She didn't have absolute reason to trust him. She'd be a fool to do that. "What else can you tell me?"

"I can't think of anything."

"Why couldn't she know Jeff?"

"Because I told her all about him, that he was a lawyer, where he worked." Sighing, her gaze skittered away. "I even described him physically and she didn't say she knew him. In fact, she was supposed to meet him and Rick at a dinner party Saturday night."

Luke stared out the window, contemplating his next move. There were guys he could call who sometimes helped him with cases. Rocky or Danny, either one would check out the hairdresser for a few bucks.

"I remembered something else."

He looked at Sydney. Hope lit her eyes.

"Julie told me Willard had her investigated. She said she'd—" She stopped abruptly, her face turning pale. "You were the one. You slept with her."

"What?"

"You were the one Willard hired. She told me about you."

"I don't know what you're talking about."

"She called you to pick me up at the salon." She stood suddenly, nearly knocking over the table as she stumbled backward. "You're in this together, aren't you? You're trying to confuse me. Trying to turn me against Willard and Rick."

"For God's sake, Sydney." He jumped up in time to

catch her before she ran out the door. "Calm down," he said, gripping her upper arms. "You're overtired and not thinking straight."

"Let go of me."

"Look at me, Sydney." When she refused, he squeezed her arms just enough to get her attention.

She gasped, her frightened gaze flying to his.

He lowered his head to look her directly in the eyes. "I was not hired to investigate Julie, and I didn't sleep with her. I didn't do that kind of tedious work for Willard."

"You investigated Rick."

"That was different. The guy claimed to be your brother. That made him an heir. That's a little bigger than worrying about a girlfriend who pops back into your life."

"Why should I believe you?" she whispered, her arms going limp.

"Stop and think for a moment. If I had any association with her, then why the elaborate charade of getting flushed out of the cabin, being chased by a helicopter? How do you explain those men showing up in Taylorville?"

Her eyes widened a fraction, and he knew the exact second her brain replayed the murder. Pain shadowed her face and she seemed to descend into darkness, her entire body going limp so that he had to hold her up.

"Come on, Sydney." He held her against his chest, concerned, helpless, angry at the feelings for her building inside him.

She tilted her head back to look at him, her lips parted and, without a second thought, he lowered his head and lightly brushed her lips with his. She whimpered softly and he increased the pressure of his mouth on hers.

When she slid her arms around his waist, he should have stopped. But he wanted to hold her tighter, delve inside her mouth with his tongue. Feel the softness of her small perfect breasts.

After the first night in the cabin, he'd seen them again and again in his dreams. He worked hard to block the image of her lowering herself into the tub. But at night, his mind betrayed him. He saw the rosy pink tips of her breasts, the indention of her waist, the flair of her curvy hips. The last time he'd managed to grab a couple of hours of sleep, he'd awoken with a hard-on so bad it ticked him off.

What was it about Sydney Wainwright that got under his skin? So what that she wasn't what he'd expected. Surely other rich girls had social consciences, used their power and privilege for good. She wasn't so special.

He started to pull away, but she clung to him, pressing her breasts against his chest, rubbing her thigh against his. She had to know what she was doing to him. He was so damn rock-hard she had to feel it.

Maybe that was the point. Get him all worked up and then bolt.

He roughly put her away from him, his breathing so ragged he could barely catch a breath. She looked at him with glassy eyes, letting her arms fall to her side as embarrassment crept into her face.

"Better get some sleep," he said, avoiding her eyes. "We'll leave early tomorrow morning."

She stepped back, wrapping her arms around herself. "Where are we going?"

He didn't answer, not sure he wanted her to know yet. But he knew exactly where they were headed. A place

he swore he'd never return. But he knew the bayous like
the back of his hand. He could keep her safe there.

If only from himself.

Chapter Eleven

Even with the windows up and the air conditioner on, Sydney felt the oppressive heat as they got closer to the swamps. Dallas could be humid. Houston often reminded her of a sauna. But the sticky dampness that clung to her skin after only a brief stop at a convenience store made her want to strip off her clothes.

She looked over at Luke. He didn't seem to be bothered by the heat. Of course, it was hard to tell. He'd barely said a word to her since they'd gotten up this morning.

Memories of last night brought more heat to her face and she tried futilely to adjust the air-conditioning vent toward her cheeks. She'd practically forced herself on him, and he'd pushed her away. Although he had kissed her first. He'd even gotten hard, so she knew he was interested. At least physically.

But then he'd obviously changed his mind.

She groaned inwardly and stared out the window at the trees dripping with Spanish moss. God, she was tired. After the awful scene, sleep hadn't come easily.

"Hand me some water."

"Don't you know how to say please?"

He slid her an amused look. "Please."

She'd finished the last of the bottles she kept up front so she twisted around to get to the cooler in the backseat. Just as she got the top open, the car swerved and she fell against Luke.

"Sorry," she murmured, grabbed a couple of bottles of Evian and settled back in her seat before handing him one.

"The road is going to get pretty rough from here." He kept one hand on the steering wheel while he uncapped the bottle. "Most of it's gravel and, depending on how much rain they've been getting, there could be some fairly deep ruts."

"You still haven't told me where we're going."

"Sure I have."

"Not specifically. Is there a particular motel you have in mind? Someone's house? Another cabin?"

He took his gaze off the rocky road long enough to lift a brow at her. "Why are you so prickly?"

"It's hot and buggy, and I think a mosquito bit me back there at the store."

He smiled. "Get used to them. Bayou mosquitoes have been known to eat alligators whole."

What had him in such a good mood all of a sudden? She liked it better when he wasn't talking to her. "So? Where are we going?"

He pulled the car off the road and drove another twenty feet where she doubted any other car had ever been. "You're about to find out," he said. "Hold on."

She tightened her seat belt and dug her heels into the floorboard as they bounced a few more yards. They finally stopped but there wasn't anything but more shrubs and trees.

"Stay here." Luke got out of the car, stopped to look around, paying particular attention to the road they'd just left.

He stood perfectly still and when she called to him, he put a finger to his lips. She waited and rolled down her window to listen, too. Nothing but the sound of birds.

He came back to the car and ducked his head inside. "I'll be back in a minute. Stay put, okay?"

She started to protest and then realized he probably needed to relieve himself, so she just nodded. Before she could find something to use to fan herself, he reappeared.

"Let's go." He opened the back door and grabbed a bag and the extra cooler of ice he'd bought at the convenience store.

"Where?"

"We're staying here for the night."

She stepped out of the car, looking around in a full circle. Nothing but vegetation. And mosquitoes. She slapped at one and missed.

"Come on. It's not far." He grabbed the cooler, closed and locked all the doors and started into the woods.

She had little choice but to hurry after him, watching where she stepped, certain something would jump out and bite her. In a matter of seconds, they came across another small clearing, only this one had a shack.

Luke looked at her, a smile lurking at the corners of his mouth. "Home sweet home."

"You're kidding."

"Just for the night."

"Why?"

"It's just a fish camp and not equipped to accommodate us any longer than that."

"No, I mean…" She stared at the way the building leaned to one side, how some of the eaves had rotted. "Why stop here at all?"

"The truth?"

She met his eyes. "Of course."

"To make sure we haven't been followed."

"Oh." She rubbed her arms, suddenly oblivious to the heat. "But if we have been followed, aren't we sitting ducks?"

"I'm pretty certain we're free and clear, but I'll camouflage the car. Besides, if anyone comes down that road, I'll hear them."

"I don't know…"

"It's got to be this way."

She didn't understand, but that didn't matter. She could see the determination in his eyes. There'd be no argument, no other option. "Okay."

He led her inside the shack, kicking an empty beer can out of her way as she crossed the threshold. The room was incredibly small, with only a cot and a wood-burning stove. Several more empty beer cans and a bread wrapper littered the wood floor.

And, God, but it was hot inside. Incredibly hot. Like an oven.

"How can we stay here?" Sydney struggled for a breath. "We'll suffocate with this heat."

"It's only May. It's not that hot yet."

"Are you insane?"

"I'll make you comfortable enough."

"Right." Sweat had gathered between her breasts

and behind her neck. "Maybe we could sleep in the car."

"And run the air conditioner all night? No way." He set down the bag and cooler. "I've got to make another trip to the car. Stay here."

"I'm going with you." She stepped over a suspicious-looking heap and unconsciously reached for his hand.

He stared down as her fingers grazed his palm. Then he looked up, their eyes meeting briefly, and she quickly pulled back.

She bit her lip, mentally calling herself every name in the book as she followed him outside. "Who would use a place like this?"

"Fishermen."

"Are we close to water?"

"About twenty yards past the shack is the swamp."

"Isn't it dangerous?"

"Sometimes."

Out of the hollow trunk of a fallen tree, a small furry animal poked its head out and then darted across the path. Sydney screamed.

Luke spun around. "What's wrong?"

She pointed. "I don't know what it was. Some kind of animal."

His gaze went to the path and he shook his head. "Nothing to worry about."

"How do you know?" she muttered, but he didn't hear. He'd barely slowed down.

He'd gotten to the car and had the trunk popped by the time she caught up. He unloaded a bag of groceries, three jugs of water and another foam cooler she hadn't realized he'd bought. She started to pick it up, but it was so heavy she took the groceries and one of the jugs instead. Then she stood back while he covered the car with branches.

After he used a large leafy branch to brush away tire marks, he motioned her to precede him down the path back toward the shack.

"Why couldn't we stay in that motel we passed about half an hour ago?" she asked over her shoulder.

"Look, Sydney, you've been doing great so far. Don't turn into a prima donna on me now."

"It was a simple question." She continued in silence, and even when they reentered the shack, she stayed quiet.

Amazingly, she found a broom and swept the floor as best she could. The cot actually had bedding on it, but it looked so disgustingly dusty she didn't even bother trying to shake it out or inspect it. She'd sleep standing up before she'd lie on that thing.

"I bought turkey and ham for sandwiches," Luke said. "Oh, and some yogurt."

"I hope that's not for me."

"You don't like yogurt?"

She shook her head and continued to prepare a clean spot for herself in the corner.

"I thought all women liked yogurt," he muttered to himself, but she heard.

She chose to ignore the sexist remark and settled herself in her corner. Except it was hot. Hot enough that she thought about sleeping outside. But it was hot out there, too.

"You'll feel better after you have a bath," he said, almost as if he'd read her mind.

"A bath?" That got her attention. "Where?"

"Where do you think?"

"You don't mean the swamp."

He smiled. "You can use two of those jugs."

She moistened her lips, the thought of cool water sluicing her heated skin almost too much to hope for.

"I swiped a towel from the motel. Take it, and find a tree. I'd do it before it gets dark."

She peered out the window. It was already dark. Twilight, anyway, but dim enough to miss a creature that might sneak up on her. She swallowed. "Will you come with me?"

"Need someone to scrub your back?"

"I'd like you to stand watch."

His lips lifted in that annoying grin that warned her he was about to say something she'd detest. "Sweetheart, I'd watch you anytime."

"Jerk." She grabbed the towel, a fresh T-shirt and one of the jugs of water. But once she stepped outside, she hesitated.

Strange sounds accosted her ears. Her gaze darted from a breeze-stirred leaf to the flight of a mosquito to the fall of moss from a tree.

Taking a deep breath, she turned around and went back inside. "I don't suppose you swiped some—"

He held up a bar of soap, and then he picked up the second jug of water. "Come on."

"I don't need your—"

He grabbed her arm as he walked past. "Let's get this over with so we can eat and I can get some sleep."

She wisely remained silent and followed him to a massive banyan tree. He set down the jug of water, handed her the soap and then went around to the other side of the trunk.

"Yell if you need me," he said. "I'll stay here until you're done."

"Thank you." She scanned the area, stepping out of her tennis shoes and shorts but leaving on her panties. "Luke?"

"Yeah."

"There could be someone around here, right? I mean, if the shack is here, it's for a reason."

"No one's here. Fishermen use it for shelter if there's bad weather."

She glanced up at the blue sky. Not a cloud in sight. Taking another look around, she pulled off her shirt and bra. She carefully set them aside and then uncapped the water. Using one hand to lather herself, she tipped the jug over her breasts. It was heavy and she wasted too much water on the first try, so she set it down and worked on lathering the rest of her body.

When she was through, she picked up the jug again. She'd just tipped it to rinse herself when something scurried across her feet.

She shrieked and dropped the jug.

"Sydney!" Luke flew around the trunk. He stopped, his gaze roaming her body. "You okay?"

She nodded. "I—I—something ran across my feet."

"Probably just a lizard." He averted his gaze and picked up the jug. "They're harmless."

"Sorry I wasted the water." She couldn't believe she was standing here with nothing on but her panties, having a normal conversation with this man. Of course, he'd already seen a good deal of her naked.

"No problem. It didn't all spill."

To his credit, he didn't so much as peek as he handed her the jug and then turned away.

"Luke?"

"Yeah." He stopped, but stayed facing away from her.

"Don't take this wrong, but I really do need my back scrubbed."

He didn't move, didn't say a word. After several seconds, he slowly turned around. At the same time, she did the same, giving him her back.

Wordlessly, he took the soap from her hands and ran the bar over her back down to the waistband of her panties. She hooked her fingers in the elastic and drew them down to mid-hip level. He followed her lead with the bar of soap, going even farther than the elastic, molding the curve of her buttocks.

She lifted her arms to push the hair off her nape, and he brought the soap up one side of her body, running his lathered hand up the other. He reached the side of her breasts and, holding her breath, she left him access with her raised arms.

His fingers grazed the sides, and she closed her eyes and swayed backward. As his fingers neared her nipples, she heard his sharp intake of breath.

He muttered a foul curse. Lowered his hands.

"Hurry up," he said harshly. "I'll wait for two more minutes."

She didn't have to wait for him to go. He disappeared in a flash, and she quickly rinsed off the suds and dried herself with the threadbare motel towel. Skipping the bra, she slipped on the fresh T-shirt and then pulled her shorts back over her wet panties.

"AREN'T YOU going to eat?"

"It's too hot." She didn't know why she'd bothered taking a bath an hour ago. Her skin was already sticky. Not that it had anything to do with her body temperature soaring to a dangerous level.

She leaned back against the wall and, using the fan she'd fashioned from a magazine cover, fanned herself with new zeal. She could barely look at Luke's hands without remembering how they felt on her breasts. Or how they'd run over the curve of her bottom.

"Fifteen more minutes and it's lights out. I'd eat something if I were you." He put a spoonful of strawberry yogurt in his mouth.

She made a face. "You like that?"

"No, but it's cold."

She sighed and fanned harder. He had a point.

"Come on. Eat half a sandwich and a carton of yogurt and I have a surprise for you."

"What?"

"Eat first."

She got up and went to the cooler, and saw that he'd already made her a turkey sandwich. She didn't bother cutting it in half. A few minutes ago, her stomach had complained about her stubbornness. Of course, it wasn't just obstinacy that drove her to sit silently in the corner. She was embarrassed over the bath incident.

Not that Luke hadn't been a willing participant, but she'd started the whole thing, and after last night...

She couldn't think about it. Any of it. Luke had been acting as if nothing had happened. She could do that, too. After taking a bite of the sandwich, she grabbed a carton of yogurt and returned to her corner.

Luke went about moving the cot, sweeping, and then pulled out a couple of sheets from his bag.

She laughed. "Did you swipe that from the motel, too?"

He gave her a dry look. "I took two towels and two sheets, and left fifty bucks on the table. I think that covered it. Now face the other way or no surprise."

She did as he asked as she finished her sandwich. Although she'd already gotten her surprise. He'd left money for the linen?

Laying her head back, she pressed one of the chilled bottles of water to the side of her neck. She'd already guzzled enough to send her to every tree in the vicinity. Thankfully, she wised up and cooled it on the liquid intake. Fortunately, with the sun down, the temperature had eased, too. Couldn't say the same for the humidity.

"You finished eating?"

She set the water bottle aside and turned around. He was kneeling on the floor where the cot had stood. On the floor were the sheets, kind of tucked in and puffy like a feather bed.

She had to be dreaming. "What's that?"

"Come see."

Sydney walked up alongside him. "I think I'm hallucinating. It looks like a bed."

"Try it out."

She made a face.

"These are the same sheets you slept on last night."

"But what's under them?"

"You won't know until you try it."

She hesitated. This had to be a trick. There could only be a hard wood floor under there.

"Okay, I'll use it. You can sleep on the cot."

She glanced at the rickety dusty thing and groaned. "I'd rather sleep sitting up."

"Suit yourself." He pulled off his boots and then slid between the sheets and sighed with exaggerated contentment. "Nice and cool."

"Cool? You're crazy."

He closed his eyes. "Switch off the lantern, will you?"

Her curiosity got the better of her and she crouched down to touch the edge of the makeshift bed. It did feel cool. But how could it?

He opened his eyes. "Change your mind?"

"Come on. What's under here?"

He flipped the sheet back in invitation. "An old fisherman's trick—a pit under the cot deep enough for a couple of blocks of ice, a sheet of plastic, a sleeping bag on top and then the sheets."

"Oh, my, God." She pressed her palms to the sheets. Cool and soft. Not waiting for a second invitation, she crawled in beside him and lay flat on her back, closing her eyes, enjoying the coolness against her skin.

"Feel good?" he whispered.

"Heavenly."

"Too bad you didn't take me up on my offer."

She opened her eyes and looked at him, his face close. Disturbingly close. "What do you mean?"

A smile lurked at the corners of his mouth. "I gave you your chance to claim it. I'm pretty comfortable now."

"Oh." He was right. Damn him. For a moment, she thought about laying on a guilt trip to make him give up the bed, but she hated to give him the satisfaction. "Okay."

She started to push herself up, but he touched her arm. "I'm kidding. Stay here."

"With you?"

"You have a problem with that?" His eyes seemed to bore into hers as he ran the back of his fingers down her cheek.

Slowly, she shook her head, her body coming to life with the promise of his touch. "Good night," she whispered.

He smiled and then kissed her. Lightly at first, but when she didn't resist, he used his tongue to part her lips. Eagerly, she received him, and when he cupped her waist with one large hand, she slid her hand up his chest to his shoulder.

Pulling back, he met her eyes. "You want the lantern off?"

"It doesn't matter." The words barely made it past her lips, her breathing had become so ragged.

"We'll leave it on." He lowered his gaze to her breasts. Her hardened nipples showed through the T-shirt. "You'd be cooler without this," he said, pinching the fabric between his thumb and forefinger.

She reached for the shirt hem, pulled it over her head and cast the shirt aside. "You, too."

The thrilling way his gaze hungrily roamed her bare breasts made her wet, and she anxiously tugged at his T-shirt. Not as gentle as she, he ripped it off over his head. The sound of the neckline tearing fueled her excitement. She reached for his belt buckle, but he held her wrists and lowered his mouth to her breasts.

He tongued each nipple until she couldn't stand it. She pitched forward and he suckled her, hard, so that she could barely breathe. He released one of her wrists and ran his hand down her belly, to her panties. The elastic waist gave as he slid his hand underneath.

Automatically, she squeezed her thighs together. He paused, retreated and then his mouth moved to hers. She parted her lips and welcomed his tongue, and then guided his hand back to the juncture of her thighs.

He needed no other encouragement. In seconds, he'd removed her panties, unbuckled his belt and slid off his jeans.

Once they were naked, Luke draped himself over her, his long, muscled body pressing her into the cool depths of the cocoon of pillows. She remembered the feel of him—the hard expanse of his chest, the corded strength of his thighs. But this time, she wasn't afraid for her life. She ran her hand down the length of his back as he cupped her breast, his mouth finding hers and making it his own.

She moaned as he plunged his tongue inside her, as his hand moved slowly down her body, brushing the skin so lightly she shivered, until he reached the patch of curls. Sydney spread her legs, wrapping one around his back as she tasted his hunger.

His fingers, not to be rushed, circled and teased as he inched lower and lower until he reached the top of her nether lips.

Each moment he delayed was torturous. It was time to take matters into her own hands. She reached between them until she grasped the thick, hard length of him. His gasp pleased her, and she rubbed him up and down, feeling him grow within her palm.

The ploy worked and his fingers slipped inside her, stroking once, twice, then finding the center of her pleasure. Gently, he circled the bud of flesh. Over and over, never increasing the pressure, never wavering from his target.

She arched her back and wallowed in the rising tide of pleasure. His low chuckle made his chest vibrate and only then did she remember she had him in her hand.

It was his own fault that she let him go. His touch was too much. She couldn't focus on anything but the way her body coiled like a spring about to snap.

She arched again, straining, and finally his rhythm changed. Still circling, he moved faster, faster, and that was it—her whole body tensed all the way down to her toes, her hands fisted the bed sheets, her head snapped on the pillow as the world narrowed to the point where his fingers met her flesh.

She screamed as she came, but he swallowed the cry with a kiss as he pushed her thighs apart with his legs. Then he plunged inside her, his thick length rubbing her just so, stretching her orgasm into a series of unbelievable spasms that rocked her to the core.

His hands moved down to lift her other leg around his back. He strained on top of her, no longer kissing, his arm muscles bunched and corded as he held himself up. Her gaze was caught on the tension in his neck, his bulging Adam's apple, but then she came again, and everything on the outside faded.

He called out once, a low guttural cry of, "Sydney…" And then, the whole weight of his muscled body pushed against her, filled her.

Finally, her hands relaxed their grip. His head came

down and their eyes met. Sweat beaded on his forehead
and ran down his temples. He smiled in that cocky way
of his, but she didn't mind. And when he kissed her, she
didn't mind that either.

Chapter Twelve

The closer they got to Mama Sadie's, the more Luke started to sweat. The heat was part of it. He hadn't been back to the swamps in seven years and the cloying mugginess was far worse than he remembered. But it was having to face Mama and Jacques that was eating at him.

They knew about him being in prison; hell, they knew everything. That didn't make it better. He'd been their golden boy. He'd done them proud once. Before he'd fallen from grace. He *hadn't* fallen. He'd been kicked. Hard to remember sometimes after the degradation he'd been through.

The burned-out shanty that lightning had struck fifteen years ago was still standing, but he didn't need the landmark to know it was time to turn. He could get to Mama's blindfolded. For eleven years, it had been the only home he'd known.

Glancing over at Sydney, still peacefully sleeping, he tried to make the turn as smoothly as possible, considering the road went from bad to worse. Gravel spun under the tires and roots from hundred-year-old trees wound like serpents close to the surface giving the light-weight economy car a hell of a workout.

His reluctance to wake Sydney wasn't altruistic. He'd been a fool last night. He never got involved with clients. For damn good reason. He knew better. Any kind of emotional attachment put them both at risk. What the hell about her had reduced him to stupidity?

He looked over at her. She looked so vulnerable, with thick lashes resting on her cheeks, her lips slightly parted, her breathing slow and steady. Even now, knowing what a mistake last night had been, he still wanted her.

Dammit all to hell.

Better she sleep and not distract him. Besides, he didn't want her asking questions. Stirring up old memories. She'd hear the stories soon enough. Not from Mama Sadie. She respected Luke's desire for privacy. She knew him like no one else did.

But the others would talk. They'd mean no harm, but that was their way. Part of life in the swamps. Mama would do her best to keep Sydney away from the gossipers, but she'd hear stories about him. Most of them true. When it came to Luke Boudreau, folks didn't have to exaggerate to weave a sordid tale.

Hell, what did he care? Sydney meant nothing to him. Last night was just great sex. Nothing more. Within a week, he'd never see her again. She'd be back in her own world of charity balls and high-powered meetings. But life would never be the same, no matter how many distractions her money provided. The bitter taste of betrayal would remain on her lips.

Luke understood all too well.

"TIME TO wake up."

Sydney felt something on her shoulder. She lifted her head and tried to open her eyes, but she didn't want the wonderful dream she was having to end. She and Luke were sitting on the beach in the Caribbean, sipping piña coladas between long passionate kisses. The sun was setting...

Someone nudged her shoulder again, and she slowly opened her eyes. She smiled at Luke.

He withdrew his hand. "We're here."

She blinked, looked around. A few yards from the car stood a large structure. Not exactly a cabin or a shack, but not a house either. "Where is here?"

Without answering, he got out and went around to the trunk, ignoring her, just as he had since they'd awoken this morning. As if last night had never happened.

Hurt and shame burned in her chest. Last night had been awesome. Phenomenal. Granted, her experience was limited, but no one had ever made her feel the way she had last night. As if she'd truly walked on a cloud, or had soared to the summit of ecstasy. Obviously, he felt differently. For him, it had been an act of release.

Screw him. She stayed where she was, sick and tired of his silent treatment. How could he have been so tender and attentive last night and so aloof today?

A creak drew her attention to the door of the building. A small child poked out his dark head and stared curiously at her through big brown eyes. Behind him, a taller girl appeared, older, in her early teens, her dark eyes wary.

Until she spotted Luke.

She opened the door wider, her eyes lighting up as she stepped onto the porch. "Uncle Luke!"

He came around the car from the trunk with a bag and cooler in each hand and immediately put them down. "Could this be—no this can't be Antoinette. The last time I saw her, she was a little girl. You're almost a woman."

Laughing, apparently mindless of her bare feet, she flew down the warped wooden stairs, holding out her arms. Luke caught her by the waist, held her in the air and swung her around.

How different he looked. Not at all like the same man with whom she'd just spent the last seventy-two hours. The warmth of his smile transformed his entire face. Weariness seemed to melt away from his eyes, changing them from icy coolness to a stunning blue.

Jealously clawed at her. That was supposed to be the way he looked at her this morning. Instead of with regret. Fine.

She could pretend nothing happened between them, too.

He finally set the girl down and pushed back her long black hair. "Antoinette, *chérie*, I can't believe how much you've grown."

She lifted her chin with a defiance that said she expected an argument. "I go by Toni now."

"Ah." Smiling, he touched the tip of her nose. "Beautiful and strong-willed. Mama must keep a shotgun by her side."

Her heart-shaped face creased in a frown. "Why would she do that?"

"To keep the boys away, *chérie*."

"Oh, Uncle Luke." She rolled her eyes, her cheeks turning pink.

"Who is that?" he asked, inclining his head toward the little boy who'd taken two more steps out onto the porch.

"His name is Diego. He came last year. He's still shy, especially around strangers."

Luke flinched. He recovered quickly, but Sydney knew she hadn't imagined his reaction. Clearly he wasn't a stranger here. Maybe the girl's remark had made him touchy.

She'd called him uncle. Was it just an endearment of respect or were they related? Sydney's curiosity got the better of her and she opened the door and stepped out of the car.

Luke looked over at her. "Sydney, come meet Antoin—" His lips twitched. "Toni."

The girl didn't smile when she whispered, "Is she your girlfriend?"

"No, she's just a friend." His eyes met Sydney's, and she got the message to follow his lead. "Sydney, this is Toni."

"Hi." Sydney approached with her hand extended. "I'm pleased to meet you."

Toni hesitated, staring at Sydney's hand before finally shaking it, a tentative smile lifting her lips. "Me, too."

"Where's Mama?" Luke asked, reclaiming the bag and the cooler.

"She went to Madame LaRue's about two hours ago." Toni slapped at a mosquito. "Did she know you were coming? She didn't say nothing."

He frowned at her with raised brows. "She didn't say what?"

Toni grinned. "Didn't say anything."

"I didn't call," he said, looking around. "I wanted to surprise her. What about Jacques? Is he here?"

"Today's the day he picks up supplies."

He nodded at something behind Sydney. "That's new."

She'd been busy watching out for the little blood-suckers that had already welted her skin in several places, but she followed his gaze to a weathered shed. Hardly new. In fact, she was surprised it was still standing. It looked like an outhouse.

The girl shrugged. "Not so new. Mama got it from Virgil Pinchot for delivering Minnie's baby last spring. She had another girl."

"What does that make—six?"

"Eight. You've been away too long." With a devilish grin, she said something else, not in English, it sounded more like French but not the kind Sydney knew.

Luke gave her a disapproving look. "English, Toni, we have a guest. Besides, would Mama like to hear you talking like that?"

With a lift of her chin, she headed back toward the porch. "I'm sixteen. Not a child anymore."

Watching her, Luke sighed and muttered, "They grow up too fast."

"Is she your niece?"

He darted a look at Sydney almost as if he'd forgotten she was there. "Not exactly. Mind grabbing the other bag?"

At his dismissal, she clenched her teeth. She had a right to know who these people were. Damn him. She went around to the trunk, got the other bag and then hurried after him. She counted today her lucky day when she didn't trip over the aged wooden steps. The little boy who'd been standing on the porch dashed inside. Toni stood holding the door open.

"There's only one spare room," she said, eyeing Sydney speculatively. "But I suppose she can sleep with me. I have two beds."

Sydney's cheeks heated. She looked away from Toni and straight into Luke's eyes. He didn't so much as blink.

"We'll work it out." He took over holding the door, stepping aside so Sydney could precede him.

Once over the threshold, she felt like Alice in Wonderland. As shabby as the outside was, the inside was neat and clean and an eclectic blend of charm. Nothing should have worked—not the three large overstuffed sofas in green and blue and yellow, forming a U shape, nor the two window seats with velvety blue and gold cushions. But they blended nicely with the varnished tree stump end tables that Sydney couldn't be sure didn't come straight from the ground through the floor.

Surprisingly large, too, the room seemed to go on forever. It kind of rambled into a kitchen that disappeared around a bend almost as if someone had decided at the last minute to add on another room.

"Something smells good in here," Luke said, sniffing the aromatic air as he set down the cooler.

"It's gumbo. But you're probably too citified now to recognize it." Toni gave him a teasing grin and then eyed the cooler. "Anything in there needs to go into the ice box?"

"Some cheese and cold cuts." He touched the tip of her nose. "You think I wouldn't recognize Mama's gumbo a mile away?"

Toni giggled. "That's how much you know. I made it."

"You?"

"Yes, me." She carried the cooler into the kitchen.

"Why aren't you in school?"

"I finished. Got my diploma two months ago."

"Good girl." Luke followed her and Sydney stayed close behind.

She wondered that he didn't seem surprised that at sixteen, Toni had already graduated. Of course, Sydney wondered about a lot of things. Like what was Luke's relationship to these people? Why had he brought her here? If they were truly in danger, surely he wouldn't endanger these people, as well.

She stopped and stared at the three sets of tables and chairs lined up in yet another offshoot of the kitchen. The place was beginning to look like a boardinghouse.

Something outside caught her attention. She moved to the window and peered through the blinds. Water stretched as far as she could see. Not the beautiful blue-green of the Caribbean that surrounded her parents' Saint Croix home where she'd spent many winters. She wouldn't so much as stick one toe in this dark, muddy abyss.

Luke came to stand alongside her and moved the blinds back. The swamp wound around through trees with trunks as big as barrels, their gnarled branches providing shade from the sun.

"It feels like we're sitting right on top of the water," she said, unable to stop the shiver that made her wrap her arms around herself.

"We are. This side of the house is on stilts."

She didn't like that idea and automatically stepped back from the window. "Why?"

Cupping her elbow, he guided her back to stand beside him. He squinted off to the west, his attention focused on something she couldn't see, the old lines of tension returning to bracket his mouth. "You'll find out in a minute."

Before she could identify the source of his agitation, she heard the distant purr of a motor. At least she thought it was a motor. She listened carefully for a moment.

Panic gripped her.

Her gaze flew to the treetops.

The helicopter. It had returned. Just as Luke had predicted.

She stumbled backward, but he slipped an arm around her shoulders and held her.

"No, Sydney. It's not what you think. Look." He pointed toward the setting sun.

She squinted like he had and saw something moving on the water. A boat. Headed toward the house.

She swallowed. "It could be them."

He smiled and squeezed her shoulders. "It's not. You're safe here."

Just that one small act of tenderness reduced her to jelly. Made her want to foolishly cling to him. He had the right attitude. Pretend last night never happened.

Behind them, a loud bang startled them both.

Toni had dropped the cooler to the floor. "I put your stuff in the ice box," she said, unsmiling. "I hear Mama. I'm going to go help her dock."

Sydney watched the girl leave by a door off the kitchen. "She has a crush on you," she said, craning her neck to see exactly where Toni was going.

"Right." Luke snorted. "I've known her since she was a year old."

Sydney watched as the girl took a short flight of stairs with amazing agility. Her long brown legs were slim and toned and perfect enough that they could be displayed on Dallas billboards.

"She's not a kid anymore. I'll bet you your fee that she has the hots for you."

Luke frowned, while watching over Sydney's shoulder as Toni flipped back her long shiny black hair and then crouched on the small wobbly-looking dock in preparation for the approaching motorboat.

If one could call it a boat. It had to be twenty years old and very likely handcrafted. An umbrella shaded the passenger and blocked Sydney's view.

"That's ridiculous," Luke muttered.

"So it's a bet?"

"You're getting on my nerves," he said and walked toward the kitchen.

"Luke, seriously…"

He hesitated at the door Toni had exited and looked at Sydney.

"Be careful with her feelings. Sixteen's a tough enough age."

He seemed annoyed. "You want to come meet Mama or not?"

"You mean climb down there?" Her gaze went to the rickety steps. "Near the water? No way."

One side of his mouth went up. "Why not?"

"No, thanks."

"You think something's going to bite you?"

"It could."

"You're right." Amusement sparkled in his eyes. "No telling what might jump out at you. An alligator, water moccasin, maybe even a piranha."

"Very funny."

He smiled and went out the door. Sydney went back to the window in time to see the boat pull up alongside the dock. A large woman wearing a wide-brimmed straw hat tossed Toni a rope, which she quickly tied to a post.

At the front of the boat an umbrella, a rocking chair and some boxes were in the way so Sydney couldn't see who else accompanied the woman. For someone so large, she stood with ease, balancing herself until she put a foot on the dock.

But then she saw Luke.

One hand went to her throat, the other waved helplessly in the air. Luke caught it and kept her from toppling. He helped her onto the dock and she grabbed him, hugging him to her enormous bosom.

Sydney still couldn't see the woman's face. Her skin was olive, her hair dark, her age undeterminable. She couldn't seem to let Luke go until he finally extricated himself. When he stepped back, the affection on his face warmed Sydney, and stirred her curiosity all over again.

Sydney felt a small tug on her shirt and she looked down into the soulful brown eyes of the little boy she'd seen earlier. He gave her a shy smile and held out a glass of water to her.

"Thank you." She accepted it and took a sip. "What's your name?"

He didn't answer, just stared back at her.

"My name is Sydney."

His lashes lowered. "Diego."

"That's David in Spanish, isn't it?"

He shrugged his slim shoulders.

"Do you live here?"

He nodded.

Sydney smiled to herself. The boy was getting a great start on manhood. Why talk when a nod or grunt would do? "How old are you?"

He shrugged again, and then asked, "Are you going to live here, too?"

"I think we'll be here for a few days," she said, surprised that he spoke without an accent. With a name like Diego, she'd jumped to a wrong conclusion.

His gaze went to the window and his eyes widened, a grin curving his mouth. "Mama's home. Sometimes she brings us a treat."

He ran for the door, and Sydney called after him, afraid for him to use the stairs or go near the water. But he ignored her and flew down the wooden steps as if he'd done it a thousand times. Which he probably had.

This was his world. Luke's world.

Sydney needn't worry about the boy. She was the one who didn't belong here.

She watched Luke, Toni and Diego unload the boat while the woman stood to the side, holding a caged chicken she'd brought with her. She wore a long skirt and long-sleeved white gauzy shirt over a red T-shirt. Far too many clothes for the stifling heat.

As the group started up the stairs, each person with an armful, Sydney realized the woman had traveled alone. She'd steered the boat through the swamps from God knows where, by herself.

The door opened, and instinctively Sydney stepped back. The boy came in first, and then Toni, who carried their bundles to one of the tables. Next, the woman entered, followed closely by Luke.

She removed her hat at the same time her eyes met Sydney's. She dropped it, the color rising in her cheeks as she whispered, "She's the one. The woman I saw in my dream."

Chapter Thirteen

Luke took one look at the fear in Sydney's face and quickly slid an arm around Mama's shoulders. He squeezed lightly, giving her a silent message. "Is that any way to greet someone?" He guided her forward. "Mama, this is Sydney Wainwright. And this beautiful woman is Sadie Boudreau. Everyone calls her Mama Sadie."

Mama laughed, but her intense gaze connected with his and he knew she had a message of her own for him. "Sydney is a very pretty name, *chérie*," she said, transferring her attention to Sydney, taking her hand and sandwiching it between her two work-roughened hands. "For a very pretty lady."

"Nice to meet you," Sydney said softly, the confusion and fear in her eyes plain.

The shared last name had to puzzle her. Although Mama was fair-skinned, no one could mistake the small portion of Creole blood that ran through her veins, giving her black hair its natural curl and her skin an olive cast.

"Come, let us have some tea." Mama started to lead her to the table in the kitchen but Luke touched Mama's arm, stopping her.

"I'll finish bringing up the boxes. Sydney might like to rest."

"As soon as we have tea, I will make a room ready, *cher*." She patted Luke's arm. "Go. Do not worry about your lady friend."

He hesitated and glanced at Sydney, who hadn't moved nor said a word. Very rarely was she speechless. He should be grateful. He'd be even more grateful if Mama kept quiet.

"No more talk of dreams, okay?" he said to her with a meaningful lift of his brows.

Sydney made a sound of disgust. "Excuse me, but I'd like to hear it."

Luke smiled. "Mama didn't really have a dream about you. She likes to tease newcomers."

Sydney didn't believe him, judging by the look on her face. No wonder. He'd just lied through his teeth. Around here, Mama was well known for her predictions, and she got paid to interpret her dreams. Luke didn't believe in that seeing-the-future stuff, even though her accuracy was pretty damn amazing.

"Uncle Luke." Toni came running from the kitchen. "That's not true. You know Mama—"

"Antoinette, Mama would love some tea. Chamomile, please, *chérie*," Mama said, making a shooing motion with her hands.

Toni didn't look happy, but she obeyed Mama, and Luke sent the woman who'd raised him a silent message of gratitude. As hard as trust came to him these days, he knew he could trust Mama not to tell Sydney anything he held private. If there was anyone in this entire world he could trust, it was her.

Hey, he'd once thought he could trust Enrique.

No, he wouldn't let his thoughts slide into that gutter. Forget the bastard. He'd already robbed Luke of enough time in this life.

Mama smiled at him. "Go about your business and leave us womenfolk to talk. Jacques will be home soon and we will have no peace in this house." Laughing, she sat in one of the kitchen chairs and clasped her hands under her breasts. "He will be surprised to see you."

"Yeah." He loved the man who'd never complained about all the children Mama had taken in over the years, but Jacques liked to talk. Too much sometimes. And since he was related to half the bayou population, sometimes discretion was a problem. "No one can know we're here, Mama. No one outside these walls."

She nodded solemnly. "Then that is how it will be."

"Thanks." He glanced at Sydney. "I won't be long and then we'll get you settled." He got to the door and hesitated. "By the way, no using the phone."

SYDNEY DROPPED a cube of sugar into her tea. She hadn't missed the look Mama and Luke had exchanged about the banning of phone calls, and Syd was still stewing over it. In essence, she was still a prisoner.

"Tell me about yourself, Sydney Wainwright." Mama smiled at her with kind hazel eyes, and Sydney bit her tongue to keep from saying something rude.

Instead, she shrugged and stalled by taking a sip of the hot tea. It was amazingly cool inside the house; not cool enough for her taste, but comfortable, considering they were situated in the middle of mosquito heaven.

"I'm not sure what you want to know," Sydney said,

wondering what Luke had told the woman. Of course, since he hadn't deemed it important to fill Sydney in, what did she care what she revealed.

Mama sipped her tea and stared pensively at Sydney. "How do you know Luke?"

"He kidnapped me."

Mama blinked and then laughter filled her eyes. "He did, eh? For any particular purpose?"

Sydney sighed. So much for the shock offensive. "He claims he was hired to protect me."

"But you do not believe him." She smiled, one of those horribly kind, understanding smiles that made you want to tell her everything.

"I have no reason to, really."

"But you are here."

"Yes." Sydney swallowed when she realized the horrible truth. She couldn't just step back into her life. Someone was after her. That much she knew for certain. "I have no place else to go."

Mama reached across the table and covered her hand. "Trust my Luke. He is a good man. If he vows to protect you, he will give his life to do so."

God, Sydney hoped it didn't come to that. She thought for a moment, trying to come up with a diplomatic way to ask the question burning in her mind. "Are you Luke's mother?"

"Not an easy answer, that one." Mama leaned back and Sydney tried not to stare at her enormous breasts. "Legally, no. In every other sense, yes."

"He lived here with you once?"

"Yes, with Jacques and me and the others."

"Jacques is your husband?"

Mama grinned, her teeth remarkably white, except for the partial gleam of gold coming from a back tooth. "Legally, no. In every other sense…"

Sydney smiled, too. "You're a modern woman. I like it."

"So are you, Sydney Wainwright." Her expression turned somber, her hazel eyes intense. "But you will marry. Very soon."

Sydney laughed. "I don't think so."

Mama only smiled and then took another sip of tea.

Toni had gone to help Luke and the little boy had disappeared down the hall. Sydney glanced around to make sure she and Mama were still alone. "What were you saying earlier about a dream?"

"More tea?" Mama pushed to her feet and ambled to the wood cookstove where Toni had left the water kettle.

Unlike the one in the shanty last night, this stove was massive, occupying the entire corner of the kitchen. "No, thanks," she said, "but I would like to know about the dream."

"Luke…" Mama waved a hand. "He doesn't like me talking about such things."

"Why?"

Mama stooped to get a huge log from the stack near the door, and Sydney jumped up to help her.

"Sit, child," Mama said and carried the log to the stove before Sydney could intercept her. "This back may be old, but it still works."

"How about I bring another one for later?" Sydney asked and picked up a log before getting an answer.

Mama gave her an approving nod and pointed to the side of the stove. She stared at Sydney a moment, as if she were measuring her in some way, and said, "I had dreams Luke would become a police officer two years before he took the test and still he doesn't believe."

"A police officer? Luke?"

Mama nodded, her face full of pride. "In New Orleans. For six years. He even became a detective."

"What happened?"

Her expression fell, and she turned away to lift the lid of a large cast-iron pot. "Antoinette started dinner. She's a good girl, that one. Strong-willed, but with a big heart." She sniffed the pot's contents. "The gumbo is almost ready. We will eat soon."

Sydney was deciding how hard to push for information when the door opened. Luke and Toni walked in. The girl's smile faded as soon as she saw Sydney.

Luke went directly to the sink and washed his hands. "We put the sacks of dried rosemary and peppers in the shed in the back. The chicken feed is near the coops." He gave Sydney a carefully noncommittal look. "You two have a nice visit?"

"Very enlightening," Sydney said, and was pleased to see alarm enter his eyes.

Grinning, Mama inclined her head toward Sydney though speaking to Luke. "She will keep your hands full."

"Not for long," he muttered.

Sydney glared at him. "One more minute would be too long."

Toni watched them with interest, her gaze darting back and forth like a ping pong ball until Mama sent her to make sure Diego was washing up.

"We have only one spare room," Mama said as soon as the girl disappeared. "Can you share it?"

Luke looked skeptically at Sydney. "I guess that would be okay."

She felt her cheeks heat up. Luckily, she wasn't prone to blushing. "How many beds?"

Mama tried to hide a smile. Even if she had been successful, her laughing eyes would have given her away. "Two."

"Fine." Sydney would never admit it, but she'd rather stay with Luke. It wasn't about the sex, although that was an excellent bonus. Absurdly, she felt safe with him. "Is there someplace where I can shower?"

When Luke and Mama exchanged amused glances, Sydney got a bad feeling.

"Antoinette will heat the water for you," Mama said, and then to Luke, "You can use Felipe's old room. You remember which one?"

"I remember." He looked out the front window, and then picked up both their bags. "Come on, Sydney."

She followed without argument, her feelings mixed about being alone with him. She had questions and he'd damn well answer them. Or she would find a way to call Willard, with or without Luke's blessing.

"*Mon ami*, it's been too long."

Startled at the sound of the unfamiliar male voice, Sydney dropped her towel. She'd been lost in the memory of last night, remembering how Luke had washed her back. "Dammit all to hell."

Outside, the talking abruptly stopped. Whoever was out there had obviously heard her. When the conversation resumed, it was in bastard French.

She didn't bother trying to listen and decipher,

mostly because she knew Luke was outside standing guard. She was more interested in salvaging her towel.

The bathhouse was small enough as it was, dimly lit with only a lantern, and the narrow wooden bench to hold her shampoo and towel hardly sufficed. She finally managed to snatch her towel, but it was too late. Half of it was soaked.

She did her best to dry off and then got into her clothes. Not really her clothes, but the ones Luke had provided—denim shorts and a white T-shirt. She made sure she was zipped up and then slowly opened the door. The mosquitoes didn't even give her a sporting chance. One dive-bombed her and she slapped at it with fervor, missing the little sucker by a mile and getting her arm.

How did people live like this? Outdoor toilets and baths. Using the swamp for transportation. Although they had electricity and plumbing, Luke explained that neither was very dependable. If she had to stay here very long, she'd go crazy.

"Come on, Sydney. Dinner's ready." Luke stood in the shadows. It was dark enough that she couldn't make out the faces of the two men with him, but she figured one was Jacques.

"*Mon dieu*, who is this lovely creature?" A shorter man stepped forward, took her hand and brought it to his lips.

Something about him unnerved her and she was about to yank it back when the other man said something in French, his tone angry, and the shorter man released her hand.

Luke stepped in between the two men. "Come on. I haven't had good gumbo in seven years."

"I feel sorry for you, my friend." The second man spoke, his accent heavy. "Let's go."

Luke steered them toward the house, while staying close to Sydney. "That's Jacques and his cousin, Bernard. I'll introduce you when we get inside."

Even from several yards away she could smell the shorter man. He reeked of rum and cigarette smoke. She didn't think that was Jacques. She sure hoped not.

They entered the kitchen to the sound of chatter and modern jazz playing softly on the radio. Mama stood at the stove stirring the pot, while Toni fed the fire with logs. Diego was setting two of the tables, along with three other children, two boys and one girl, around the eight-to-ten age range. Mama's wards, as Luke had explained earlier.

He introduced her to the two men and, thankfully, she was right—the drunk was Bernard. He didn't make it to dinner. Jacques took him to a back room to pass out and the rest of them sat down to a dinner of gumbo and rice and homemade bread and a wild berry cobbler for dessert. Sydney couldn't remember when anything had tasted better or the dinner conversation been more lively and interesting.

As soon as the plates were cleared and the children sent to the reading room along with Toni, Luke got down to business and laid out the situation. He didn't go into detail, but he didn't pull any punches, either.

"If you want us to leave, I'll understand," he told Mama and Jacques, "but you know I'd never put you and the children in danger."

"No chance they could have followed you?" Jacques asked, his swarthy face creased in a frown.

"Of course there's always a chance, but we purposely spent the night at the old fish camp just off the highway. I figured if they had followed, they would've made a move then."

At the mention of last night, Sydney grabbed her glass and took a messy sip. Water sloshed the front of her T-shirt. Her gaze automatically slid to Mama, who watched her with a knowing look that further disconcerted Sydney.

"I agree," Jacques said. "These men, doubtful they know the swamps. It is best for you to stay here."

"Of course it is," Mama said. "We would know if any strangers arrived."

Luke reached across the table and affectionately covered her hand with his larger one. "Just for a couple of days while a buddy tracks a lead for me."

Sydney stared at him. He hadn't said anything to her about having a lead.

"As long as the children are not in danger, you stay as long as you want, *cher*." Mama squeezed his hand. "It's good to have you home."

He smiled at her and then transferred his gaze to Jacques. "Is Bernard going to be a problem?"

"I don't know." Jacques expression turned grim. "You should have called. I would have kept him away."

Mama waved a hand. "He will probably remember nothing. Jacques, you take him home tonight. When he wakes up tomorrow, his head will be pounding like the devil. He will only think about getting drunk again."

Luke stared off into space, his frown thoughtful. "Maybe it would be better to keep him here."

"I am not so sure, *mon ami*." Jacques's eyebrows

went up and one side of his mouth curved. He tossed a glance at Sydney and then said something in French that made Luke visibly tense.

Sydney recognized enough of what he'd said to know that Jacques had said something about her, something about her being too pretty. She felt the heat creep into her cheeks just as she met Mama's watchful eyes.

"We could keep him drunk," Luke said, and Jacques laughed.

"I could mix him a potion," Mama said thoughtfully, her gaze drawn to a rack of herbs drying on the window-sill above the kitchen sink. "Nothing too strong."

"That's okay, Mama," Luke said quickly. "I think you're right. He's so drunk he'll be too busy hurting to worry about why I'm back."

"Two guys fishing for loblolly-bay made camp close to the Alderette shack," Jacques said. "I could have them look out for strangers and alert us."

Luke frowned. "You know these men?"

"Yeah, I know them, *mon ami.* For a fifth of whis-key, they will ask no questions."

Luke nodded. "Okay. If anyone they don't know tries to come down this road, we can leave by the swamp."

Sydney straightened. "What?"

At her sharp tone, all eyes drew to her.

"What do you mean leave by the swamp?"

Luke sighed. "Don't worry. It won't come to that."

"I'm not getting anywhere near that swamp."

"Fine. Sorry I brought it up."

Sydney swept a sheepish look around the table. "I know you people depend on the swamp for food and transportation, and I don't mean to sound disrespectful."

Feeling helpless and foolish, she shrugged. "I don't even like the ocean."

They all looked at her as if she were crazy.

"I mean, I like to look at it, but I don't go in the water. Not anymore," she murmured.

Luke's brows drew together. "Can you swim?"

"Of course I can swim. As a kid I spent most of my summers on a boat or an island."

Mama and Jacques exchanged puzzled glances.

Sydney tensed. She didn't have to explain herself to these people. And then her eyes met Luke's and she said quietly, "My parents died in a boating accident."

"I am so sorry, *chérie*." Mama reached across the table for Sydney's hand. "How horrible for you."

Jacques shook his head in sympathy. "Yes, but you need not fear the water. Your parents had an accident."

She gently withdrew her hand from Mama's and gave them a weak smile. They were just trying to help, but they didn't understand. How could they?

"Sydney?" Luke waited for her to look at him. "Were you with them?"

She pressed her lips together and slowly nodded.

"*Mon dieu*." Mama put a hand to her throat. "You were not hurt?"

"Not too badly. I was aft and they were at the helm when we collided with another yacht. I was in the hospital for a few days with a concussion and two broken ribs." She cleared her throat. "But I was released in time to attend their funeral."

"Ah, *chérie*, it is no wonder you fear the water." Jacques pushed away from the table. "I will see about carrying Bernard home." He winked at Luke. "Maybe stop at the store on the way, buy him a small bottle of scotch whiskey for his ailing head tomorrow."

Luke nodded absently, but said nothing. He seemed preoccupied. Probably because she'd just thrown a wrench into his escape plan.

Mama also got up from the table. "The children are too quiet," she said, with a knowing smile. "They think maybe I have forgotten it is their bedtime."

They both disappeared down the hall, an odd couple for certain. Physically, anyway. He was as thin as she was broad, and half a head shorter. But like Mama, Jacques had kind eyes and a ready smile. The affection they felt for each other and the children was as plain as the full moon glowing outside the kitchen window.

"Tired?" Luke asked. He seemed more relaxed. His expression had softened, and his eyes… God, they were the most incredible blue…

"A little." She glanced after Mama and Jacques. "They're nice people."

He nodded, a fond smile lifting the corners of his mouth. "They are that."

Thinking about the way he'd smiled at her last night, her tummy fluttered. "Your accent is more pronounced since we got here."

His smile faded.

"I like it," she added quickly. "I'd wondered but couldn't place it."

He made a motion with his chin. "Out there beyond the swamps, it's better to sound like everyone else. A hint of Cajun is like a Southern drawl. Sometimes people mistake the accent for stupidity."

She laughed softly. "I don't think anyone would ever mistake you for stupid."

He gave her a long searching look before scraping back his chair and getting up. "Get some sleep. You know where the room is."

"Where are you going?" She twisted around to track his movement toward the kitchen door.

"Outside to get some fresh air."

Out there? Fresh air? Was he kidding? Wisely, she said nothing, but the thought made her shiver as she watched him leave quietly and then listened to him go down the wooden stairs.

Sydney sat by herself and stared out at the moon. It was peaceful around here, she had to admit. And Mama had created a remarkably comfortable home out there in the middle of nowhere. More than comfortable, it was a true home with all the loving touches from the hand-sewn quilts hung over the back of the couches to the handmade place mats on the table.

She studied the place mats in front of her more closely and smiled when she realized Diego had crafted the piece with fall leaves under a coat of shellac and then signed the corner.

These people didn't deserve any trouble brought on them because of her. Neither did Luke. He wasn't responsible for her anymore. Not now that she understood the scope of the problem. No amount of money was worth him risking his life for her.

She had to take responsibility. That meant getting hold of Willard.

Chapter Fourteen

Luke stood on the dock and stared into the mist that hovered over the swamp like a nursing mother. The bright moon shone through the tupelos and cypress, draped heavily with Spanish moss, and cast shadows over the water.

He supposed he could understand why Sydney was afraid of the swamps. She was unfamiliar with the throaty croak of the bullfrog or the chorus of crickets that echoed through the pines and sweet gum trees. To him, it was as familiar as the stench of prison in his head, as the resentment he'd worn like a bulletproof vest for the past two years.

The assault of memories ambushed him, memories of Enrique's sudden disappearance, the short degrading trial, the shackles being slapped around Luke's ankles and waist, the humiliation…

Stop, he wouldn't go there. Couldn't afford to. Not when he was so close to getting even.

The door opened and he turned around to see Sydney standing tentatively at the threshold. She started to step outside, but then stopped.

"You need something?" he asked, not meaning to sound so curt.

"I wanted to talk."

"About?"

She studied the stairs and then gazed out toward the swamp. The moon cast an eerie glow on the water. Something moved, probably a mallard or a Southern spring peeper, and Sydney took another step back. "Never mind. I'll wait until you come inside."

Luke sighed. He could stay where he was and she'd be too afraid to come down and bother him. Or he could meet her at the top of the stairs. Sighing again, he said, "Wait."

Taking two stairs at a time, he got to the top just as she started to go back inside. He caught her hand. "We'll sit right here on this top step."

She didn't look pleased but nodded and gingerly made her way out, holding on to the rail as if her life depended on it. He'd known her parents had died in an accident, but he'd assumed it was automobile-related. Still, it was hard for him to understand fear of water. Especially when it had been his lifeline at one time.

"How old is this structure?" she asked as she slowly lowered herself to the top step.

He couldn't help but smile. "Old enough to have weathered a hundred storms. You're safe here."

She sent him a skeptical look before turning her gaze toward the water. "There is a certain feral beauty to the place."

He sat beside her, leaving as much room as he could between them. Even the faint scent of her honeyed skin drove him crazy. "Interesting description."

She turned sharply to him. "I meant that as a compliment."

"Did I say otherwise?"

"You've been so damn defensive ever since—" She looked away.

He knew she meant last night. "Look, I have a lot on my mind, like keeping us alive. Don't take everything personally."

"Of course it's personal." She met his eyes. "You're in danger because of me. Your family is in danger. I don't care what kind of precautions you've taken, I can't stay here and put everyone at risk. How could I live with myself if anything happened to these people?" Her voice cracked. "Or to you?"

Luke swallowed hard. Damn her. She was supposed to be different. Uncaring. Self-centered. Pampered. "Look, I accepted the job of protecting you. Let me worry about it."

She shook her head. "No, this isn't the job you took. This is a whole different story." She paused. "What about Mama and Jacques and Toni and the children? They didn't sign up for this."

He rubbed the back of his neck. He wouldn't let her make him feel guilty. This was his best course of action. "I told you to let me worry about it."

She turned her attention back toward the water and sighed loudly. "How are you related to Mama and Jacques?"

He knew the question was coming. Though it took her longer than he'd expected. "She found me running the swamp and took me in. Jacques came to live with us a year later after he and Mama met through mutual friends. He's only fourteen years older than me, but he's been like a father."

Sydney stared expectantly for a moment and then started laughing.

"What?"

"You think the explanation ends there?"

He exhaled loudly. "Women."

"Sexist."

He smiled. "What else do you want to know?"

"How old were you? Where are your birth parents? And what did you mean by 'running the swamp'?" She smiled. "And that's just for starters."

"Oh, brother."

"Ah, yes, siblings. How many?"

He shook his head. "I should've made you come down to the dock."

"Don't pretend to be gruff with me. I know better."

Of course she was teasing, but he didn't like the direction her thoughts had gone. Damn but he didn't want to talk about last night, but he didn't want her thinking it had meant anything or that there'd be a repeat.

He shouldn't have agreed to share a room. Even now, the almond scent that seemed to cling to her skin got to him. He thought about her too much when he should be figuring out how to expose their stalker.

"Luke?"

He snapped out of his reverie and looked at her.

"Please don't give me the silent treatment."

He mentally shook his head. What did he have to lose? Maybe if he gave her the whole sordid story, she'd realize how different they were. How after this was over, they'd have nothing in common. How she'd have no use for his kind.

"Okay," he said finally, "you want to know about me? Running the swamps means that I was a runaway living off the land and water. I was about nine, maybe ten. The woman who gave birth to me was a whore down in the French Quarter in New Orleans."

He paused, waiting for a response, an expression of shock, or a gasp of disgust, a moan of pity. He got nothing. Sydney just looked at him, as if he were reciting a grocery list.

"She had no idea who my father was, and I've never been interested enough to try and find out. I went to school when I felt like it, stole food when I was hungry and she was too drunk or busy with johns to remember she had a kid." He shrugged. "One of her johns beat me up pretty badly. That's when I headed for the swamps. Another whore's kid had told me about a small community of runaways out here, and I figured anything was better than scavenging food out of fast-food Dumpsters and smoking discarded cigarette butts."

Sydney tried not to show any emotion. She could tell he was trying to shock her. His challenging tone and defensive body language practically dared her to react. But it wasn't easy keeping her feelings to herself. Her heart ached for the little boy Luke described with such calculated indifference.

He stared out over the water, letting silence lapse for several minutes before he said, "So now you know."

She forced a laugh. "You think you're finished? How did Mama find you?"

An unexpected grin tugged at his lips. "She caught

me and another boy trying to steal eggs from her chicken coop."

"Ah, I bet you got a heck of a spanking."

"Actually, she dragged us inside and fed us the best breakfast I'd ever had." His grin turned wry. "And then she made us clean the coop. Told us we didn't have to steal to eat. There were plenty of chores to earn our meals."

He shrugged. "The next day, I came back and asked what else I could do to get lunch. I never left after that. I moved into one of the rooms, and got to stay on the condition I agreed to be homeschooled. Mama had already taken in two other boys and gave three hours of lessons every day. We all got our GEDs by the time we were sixteen."

"That's amazing." Sydney remembered being surprised that Toni had already finished high school. "She's an incredible woman. Is she the one who encouraged you to join the police force?"

He gave her a sharp look. "Who told you?"

"Mama," Sydney said slowly, confused by his annoyance. "She's proud of you."

He snorted. "What else did she tell you?"

"Nothing. That's why I'm out here bothering you."

At her teasing, not even a hint of a smile touched his lips. He simply stared in sullen silence at the moon's reflection on the water.

"Why did you quit?"

"I didn't." He gave her an unsettling smile. "I was fired, arrested and then thrown in prison."

"I already know about you going to prison, but I don't know why."

He muttered a curse. "She told you that, too?'

"You did. When you first kidnapped me and wanted to intimidate me into submission."

He reared his head back in surprise.

"Don't worry, it worked. I was terrified not knowing what you were going to do to me."

Pushing a hand through his hair, he almost looked apologetic. "I forgot I'd mentioned prison."

"Well, you did, so what happened?" She almost wished the light from the kitchen wasn't shining on him. Pain and anger collided on his face. Her heart twisted as she watched him struggle for control.

"I was framed for bribery and corruption." His laugh was humorless. "A week after I'd received a medal for valor. In fact, it was the second one I was awarded that year, not that it mattered."

"Obviously, they eventually realized you were innocent."

"Yeah, but not until I'd spent a year in prison right next to some of the scum I'd put there."

"Oh, God." Sydney put a hand to her throat. Being in prison had to be horrendous enough, but a cop in prison? She hadn't considered that horrible aspect.

He laughed again, and looked away. "Oh, yeah, it was like Christmas every day for some of those guys."

She wanted to ask what he meant, but she didn't want to know either. And she doubted it would do him any good to talk about it. Instead, she laid a hand on his arm. "At least you were finally exonerated."

"Too bad the stench never left."

"You mean some people still think you're guilty?"

He looked at her, his lips curving into an acerbic

smile. "I could have been. All the evidence pointed to me. Why should they have thought otherwise?"

"Anyone who knew you would know better." She sputtered, the mere thought he'd accept a bribe incomprehensible. "I've only known you for four days and I wouldn't believe you were guilty for a second."

He gave her the oddest look—kind of surprised, kind of pleased. "I wish you'd been on the jury."

"Me, too." She surprised herself with her own indignation, her unshakable faith that Luke would never do anything so dishonorable. Where had that belief come from? She'd only known him for four days, for goodness' sake. And during most of that time she'd been convinced he was a kidnapper.

When had her feelings changed? When he'd made her stay in the car and went after the helicopter? When he'd crawled over to the backseat to comfort her? When she'd learned that he'd left money for the sheets and towels he'd taken from the motel?

Actually, she didn't think it was any particular incident that had turned the tide. The accumulation of events that had revealed Luke's character had given her second thoughts. Made her come to believe he was the man he claimed to be. And more. Much more. He didn't have to risk his life for her. He could have cut her loose when the stakes had risen, left her to her own devices.

After they'd spent several minutes in silence, Luke staring out over the water while her mind worked overtime reviewing the information he'd told her, she yawned and stretched out her back.

He looked over at her. "Tired, huh?"

"Not really."

He smiled. "Exhausted?"

Sydney laughed. "That's much more accurate." She paused.

"Luke?"

The way he tensed made her wonder what he thought she was going to say.

She relaxed her leg so that it lightly brushed against his. "When they found out you were innocent, surely they offered you your job back."

"They did."

"But you didn't want it?"

His eyebrows came down in a fierce frown. "Are you kidding? The way those stupid bastards treated me? I wouldn't even waste my spit on them."

"You mean fellow cops?"

"Everybody." He shook his head. "You think you know someone until—never mind. Ancient history, as they say."

She bit her lip to keep from saying anything more. It wasn't ancient history to him. She could tell by the anger in his voice, the tension emanating from his body like heat from the sun.

"Well," she finally said, lifting her chin. "Screw them."

He looked at her and laughed. Really laughed. "Sydney Wainwright, sometimes you amaze me." He got up and held out his hand. "Come on. Let's go to bed."

THE ROOM WAS sparsely but cheerfully decorated with a bright red-and-yellow quilt on the double bed and a brown-and-gold tapestry on the wall. The designer who decorated Sydney's suite would have a cardiac arrest over the mismatched colors and woods, but Sydney warmed to the room immediately.

"Not the Ritz," Luke said, watching her study a small music box that looked as if it had been whittled by hand. "But you'll be safe here."

His voice sounded huskier than usual. But the excitement building inside her may have deceived her ears. Or maybe he was aware as she of the double bed they would share.

She silently cleared her throat. "The Ritz has nothing on this room." She picked up a paperweight. A polished stone with the tiniest scene of a man fishing painted on the top. "There is some incredible craftsmanship here. Do you know who did this?"

He walked up to her and her heart flip-flopped. Taking the paperweight out of her hand, he studied it for a moment and then shrugged. "Could have been any one of the kids. Or Mama herself."

It was hard to think about paperweights or anything else with him standing so close. Sitting on the steps outside was different. Here, the bed seemed to scream at her. Her body vividly remembered his touch. Craved it. "The kids?"

"She taught us all how to paint." He set the rock back on the scarred oak dresser.

"Painting is one thing, but this is an art form in itself." She truly was interested in the incredible detail, but she was glad for the distraction, too.

When she looked up again, Luke's heated gaze seared her with its intensity. A bad case of nerves made her body tingle and she stuffed her hands inside her pockets before they started to shake.

She didn't want him to think she expected a repeat of last night. Although truthfully, all he had to do was crook his finger and she'd strip him down to nothing. God, when she got back to Dallas she'd have to start seeing her therapist again. This sudden hunger for him couldn't be healthy. She barely knew him. She didn't attach herself to men that easily.

The thought of returning to Dallas suddenly sounded absurdly foreign. Images of her penthouse office, the mansion she'd inherited from her parents, the apartment she kept downtown...they all seemed like they belonged in another lifetime. To another person.

"What are you thinking about?" he asked, his voice low as he nudged her chin up.

"Home."

Disappointment flickered in his eyes, and he lowered his hand. "You'll be home soon. I spoke to someone in Dallas earlier. Rocky's good. He'll get back to me by tomorrow."

"And then what?"

His lips curved in an icy smile that made her shiver. "And then I turn the tables on the bad guys."

"Promise me you won't do anything dangerous."

"Don't worry. You'll be safe here."

"I'm not worried about me."

He met her eyes and trailed her cheek with one finger. "Maybe you should be," he whispered.

"Luke, promise me."

He lowered his head and briefly brushed her lips with his, and she closed her eyes but tried not to give in to the heady sensations making her knees weak, making her want to lie down and let him bury himself in her. She would, later, but right now she wanted to make sure he wouldn't do anything stupid. If she could get him to give his word...

He slid his tongue between her lips and pulled her body against his. He was hard already, and she'd grown incredibly damp between her thighs. In another minute, she'd be lost. She wouldn't be able to think clearly...

"Luke..."

Groaning, he molded his hands to the swell of her buttocks and pulled her harder against his arousal. He murmured something in French that she couldn't understand and then deepened the kiss. His heart pounded against the palm she'd flattened on his chest.

She had to stop him. Make him understand that he couldn't play avenger. That the matter should be turned over to the police. They could both stay in protective custody until the men were found. If he wanted, she'd even be willing to leave the country with him. God, but she couldn't bear to see him hurt.

He slid his hands under the hem of her T-shirt and up her back, kneading and massaging as he went. When he moved his hips against her, his erection prodded her, tempted her to forget about talking, about making him promise to stay safe.

Clinging to her last shred of self-control, she reared her head back trying to break the kiss and pushed against his chest until he released her. He looked dazed as he stepped back and let his arms fall to his side.

"Luke, we have to talk." She reached out to touch his arm, but he jerked away.

"I'm sorry," he said, shoving a hand through his hair and taking another step back. "I didn't mean for that to happen."

"No, I'm not upset about you kissing me or—" Panic gripped her as she watched his expression shut down as he emotionally retreated.

His eyes had turned that icy blue she dreaded. "You stay in the room. I'll grab one of the couches."

"No, please, that's not what I meant." She put a hand out to him, but he'd already gotten as far as the door. "I only wanted to talk about tomorrow."

"Go to sleep, Sydney," he whispered, and left without allowing her to utter another word.

Chapter Fifteen

The smell of frying ham and baking bread greeted Sydney the next morning. Hard to believe she could be hungry after all she ate last night, or after how little sleep she'd gotten, but the aroma of the bread alone was enough to lure her to the kitchen.

She heard someone clanging pots and then, *"Cet homme-ça a jamais travaillé un jour de son vie."*

It was Mama's voice and Sydney, pleased that she could understand most of the peculiar Cajun-flavored French, stopped in the middle of the hall to listen and let her ear become accustomed to its nuance. The conversation wasn't personal. Mama was talking about some guy who she claimed hadn't worked a day in his life.

"Ça boit et cufume et ça couche au serin," she said while clanging more pots and pans, her annoyance clear in her tone. "Sometimes, Jacques, you do not use the brains the good Lord gave you."

Sydney still didn't know about whom she was talking, only that he stayed out drinking all night, if she understood correctly. But that Mama appeared angry with

Jacques changed things and Sydney continued down the hall to make her presence known.

Right before she entered the kitchen, Jacques muttered something about Luke that Sydney missed.

Mama grunted and said, "*Il écoute pas personne parce qu'il est amoureux.*"

Sydney stopped in her tracks.

He doesn't listen to anyone because he's in love? Was Mama talking about Luke? Sydney's heart pounded in her ears. Maybe she'd misunderstood, hadn't translated correctly. Who could Luke be in love with? He hadn't been back to the swamps in years.

Unless Mama meant her. Ridiculous. They'd slept together only one night and Sydney's imagination was already going haywire. Luke didn't love her. He'd simply been hired to protect her. She'd be a fool to confuse his concern for personal feelings.

Mama turned around and saw her, and immediately broke into a smile. Of course, she had no idea that Sydney spoke and understood French, and Sydney did her best to return the smile and not let on that her knees were about to buckle. She reminded herself again that she'd be a fool to fantasize about Luke and love and happy ever after.

Wouldn't she?

"Come." Mama exchanged a brief look with Jacques, and motioned Sydney toward the stove. "We have good strong coffee and fresh cream. Your breakfast will be ready in five minutes."

Jacques sat at the table closest to the kitchen, sipping from a steaming mug. He nodded to her, the amusement on his face a little unsettling.

"Please, don't go to any trouble," she said to Mama. "If you don't mind, I'll just make myself some toast."

Mama's eyes rounded in outrage. "Toast? That's not enough. I made biscuits and ham and grits." She made a shooing motion with her hand. "Get some coffee and sit down."

Jacques smiled and shrugged.

Sydney knew better than to argue and got a mug off the wooden rack near the stove. "Have you seen Luke this morning?" she asked nonchalantly.

Jacques stood. "He is outside on the phone. I will let him know you are asking for him."

"No," she said a little too quickly. "I was just wondering."

Heat crept into her face and she turned to pour her coffee, but not before she saw Mama and Jacques exchange knowing smiles. So what? Let them think what they wanted.

She added a dollop of cream to the thick black brew. What did she care? In a few days, she'd never see them again. Nor would she see Luke. The thought stung. Her mind raced. It wasn't as if they'd have no reason to see each other. There would be police reports and an additional investigation. Or she could always hire him. Just like Willard had done. She grimaced at her own thoughts. How pathetic would that be?

She had to really concentrate to keep her hand steady. Because she could rationalize all she wanted, but the truth was, she hoped Mama was right.

Jacques set down his mug near the sink. "Well, I will check on Bernard, and then warn Luke that he is here."

"Bernard?" Sydney stared at him. Luke wasn't going

to like this. Remembering the slimy way Bernard had greeted her last night, neither did she. "But you took him home."

Jacques sighed. "He wandered back early this morning."

"Still drunk." Mama dried her hands on the towel with angry jerky motions as she glared at Jacques. "Get rid of him. Or I will."

Sighing again, he pulled a cigarette out of his breast pocket as he went out the door.

"I don't want to cause any trouble," Sydney began, but Mama waved off her protest.

"I don't like him being here. He's a bad example for the children." She pulled on an oven mitt and opened the oven door. The mouthwatering aroma of biscuits filled the kitchen. "He's Jacques's cousin, so sometimes I overlook that he's a pig." Shaking her head, she brought a tray of fluffy golden biscuits out of the oven. "Jacques has a big heart, but has no sense when it comes to his family."

"Most people don't," Sydney said wryly. "May I help?"

"You can set the table. The plates are there." She pointed to a cupboard to the right of the sink.

Sydney took a quick sip of coffee and then got to work. "How long have you known Jacques?"

"Let's see…" Mama frowned. "Luke is thirty-one. He was nine when he first came to live here. Jacques moved in a year later. So that would be twenty-one years."

Sydney smiled. "I take it you don't celebrate anniversaries."

Mama's eyebrows went up. "Every day we spend

with people we love is a celebration, *chérie*. Each one should be cherished." Nice way of looking at life, Sydney thought as she watched the older woman use a spatula to move the biscuits to a napkin-lined basket. It was hard to tell her age. With her clear smooth skin and lively step, she seemed young, even with the liberal amount of gray streaming through her curly black hair. No telling whether she was fifty-five or sixty-five.

Almost as if she'd read Sydney's mind, Mama shook her head. "Twenty-one years. *Mon dieu*, the time goes so fast. It seems like only last week when I caught Luke—" She stopped herself, and pulled off the oven mitt.

"He told me about trying to steal your eggs."

Mama looked surprised. "He's a very private person. He doesn't like talking about himself or the past."

"I know." Sydney hesitated, not wanting to push, but her desire to learn more about him was stronger. "He told me about being framed and going to prison."

Mama's expression darkened. "That was so wrong. It nearly killed him." She shook her head, looking so distraught, Sydney was sorry she brought up the subject. "He changed after that. He is evil, that one," Mama said, her face turning angry. "He will burn in hell."

"The man who framed him?"

"Enrique." She nodded. "His partner."

Sydney gasped. "His partner framed him?"

Again, Mama nodded, this time giving Sydney a wary look before returning her attention to turning over the sizzling ham.

"He told me about it," Sydney quickly assured her. "I just never thought to ask who'd framed him. God, how awful." She thought about Vicky, one of the secretaries in her office. "I know a woman married to a cop and she complains that her husband spends more time with his partner than her."

Mama sighed, turned off the burner and motioned her toward the table. "Breakfast can wait. Let's not waste our precious privacy."

Sydney took her mug with her and followed, her heart starting to race like when she knew instinctively that something was about to happen. She sat across from Mama and watched the older woman worry her full lower lip before raising earnest eyes to meet Sydney's gaze.

"Luke didn't have an easy life as a child," she began slowly, tentatively, clearly still struggling with the decision to discuss Luke.

Sydney nodded, trying to reassure her. "I know about his mother being a prostitute and him running the swamps."

Again, surprise flickered in Mama's eyes. "He's been very truthful with you." Her lips curved in a contented smile. "I shouldn't be surprised. It was in my dream." She glanced over her shoulder toward the kitchen door. "You're the one."

"Yes, go on."

Her eyes glittered with excitement. "The one who captures Luke's heart."

Sydney's pulse leaped. "I don't understand."

Mama laughed softly. "Ah, but you do."

Sydney blushed. "You're wrong about this."

"No, even if I hadn't had the dream I would know. I see the way he looks at you. And because of you, he has swallowed his pride and come back to the swamps."

"What do you mean by swallowed his pride? He has nothing to be ashamed of. He was framed."

"True. But you don't understand Luke. Or the relationship he had with Enrique." Anger flashed in her eyes. "That boy spent weeks at a time here like he was one of my own. When they got older, together he and Luke planned their careers. Luke wanted to go to college first, and Enrique wanted to join the police force right away. After two years at the university, Luke gave in to him and dropped out. Five years later, Enrique repaid him with a knife in the back."

Sydney didn't know what to say. She felt sick inside that a friend had betrayed Luke to such a horrible extent. No wonder he was so distrusting. No wonder he could believe Willard wanted her dead.

"And for what he sent Luke to prison?" Mama made a spitting sound. "Money to pay his gambling debts. My heart still grieves."

"I can't imagine how Luke must have felt." Briefly closing her eyes, Sydney wanted to cry. She wasn't the type to get weepy, but the stress of the past four days and what she'd just learned about Luke made her want to lay her head in her arms and bawl her eyes out.

"*Chérie*, I'm sorry I made you sad." Mama got up from her chair and came around the table to put an arm around Sydney's shoulders. "I know it hurts to see the ones we love in pain, but Luke has you now. Things will get better."

Sydney started to protest, point out she was only a client, that they had no personal relationship. But the heaviness in her heart told her that was a lie. She didn't know when it had happened, but she'd fallen for Luke.

Fallen hard. Hard enough that she wanted to erase all the pain in his life. Show him that he could trust again.

That he could trust her.

"Now, I think breakfast has waited long enough." She gave Sydney's shoulders another squeeze before returning to the stove. "Luke will come looking for something to eat soon and better he doesn't catch us whispering at the table." Mama chuckled. "He pretends to be so gruff."

Sydney smiled, knowing what she meant, and quickly rose to help. "What can I do?"

"The food is done, but you can put the honey in the microwave for a minute. Luke likes it warm with his biscuits."

Sydney hadn't noticed the microwave sitting on a cart way back in the corner. Strange appliance to see in this kitchen with the ancient wood cookstove and icebox.

"Luke bought that for me," Mama said, as if reading her thoughts. "The washer and dryer, and the freezer chest, too. Ever since he left, he's sent money, even when I tell him not to waste it that way. He tried to buy me a stove and oven, too, but I'm too old to learn to cook on one of those modern contraptions."

Sydney smiled as she poured honey out of the gallon jug into a small ceramic pitcher. Nothing about Luke surprised her anymore. He was a man with many facets, all of them so appealing she knew it was hopeless. She was a goner.

"A man could starve around here." Luke came through the kitchen door, eyeing Mama with gruff affection. "When's breakfast?"

Mama swatted him with a dish towel. "As soon as you wash your hands."

His gaze went to Sydney. "Good morning. Sleep well?"

"Fine." She noticed the cell phone in his hand and tamped down her eagerness. Maybe she ought to demand he allow her to use it. After all, she wasn't a prisoner. Of course, he may have found out something that would make the point moot. "Any news?"

"Possibly. I have to make another call in a half hour. I'll know more then." He set the phone aside, turned on the sink faucet and lathered his hands with soap.

Sydney eyed the phone. After what she'd learned about Luke's horrible past experience, now she understood why he was so paranoid, why he might suspect Willard. But he was wrong, and with one phone call she could take care of everything.

He finished washing his hands and turned off the water. She quickly transferred her gaze from the phone to him.

"Luke, try this sausage gravy." Mama stood at the stove, stirring the thick white contents of a pot. She dipped a spoon into the mixture and held it out for him. "Tell me if you want more heat."

While he sampled the gravy, Sydney inched closer to the phone.

"You used the spicy sausage," he said after sampling the gravy. He frowned, but the twitch at the corner of his mouth gave him away. "I'm not sure I like it. I'd better try it again."

Chuckling at the old ploy, Mama pushed him aside. "Go get a plate. The biscuits are on the stove."

He went to the cupboard, and while his back was turned, Sydney grabbed the phone off the counter and slid it into her pocket. She waited until he was busy filling his plate and slipped out of the kitchen.

LUKE DUG INTO breakfast. He wondered what had her particularly jumpy. He waited until Mama had chewed her bite of ham and then asked, "What were you and Sydney talking about when I came in?"

She shrugged her plump shoulders. "This and that. Nothing important. Have another biscuit."

He shook his head. "I haven't seen Jacques today."

"No?" Mama looked up from stirring her coffee and then frowned. "Bernard is here."

"What?" Luke pushed back from the table, his temper rising.

"Eat. Jacques took him home last night, but he was still drunk and wandered back some time early this morning. He is hopeless, that one."

"Shit!"

"Luke." Mama gave him a stern look. "Jacques will take care of his cousin. Finish your food."

Luke didn't like it. Bernard was trouble. Everyone thought he was a harmless drunk. Luke knew better. "He hasn't been near Sydney, has he?"

"Who?" She appeared from down the hall, smiling. "I'm starved."

"There you are. You haven't eaten yet." Mama started to rise, but Sydney motioned for her to stay seated.

"I'll help myself if it's all right." She hurried to the cupboard and got down a plate, a couple of times glancing over her shoulder at them.

Uneasy, Luke watched her. He thought she had already eaten. That's why she'd disappeared. What was she up to? She was still a little jumpy, but awfully damn cheerful.

"May I get anyone anything?" she asked as she got her half-filled mug from the table and then topped it off with more coffee.

"I'll take more of that," Luke said and lifted his mug.

She smiled and brought the pot to the table. As she stepped away from the counter, he noticed his cell phone lying there. He'd forgotten to pick it up. She probably thought she could snatch it without him knowing.

Smiling to himself, he waited until she poured the thick brew into his mug and then said, "On your way back to the table, bring my phone."

"If you say please."

Mama chuckled.

"Please," he muttered, surprised Sydney didn't seem disappointed that he remembered the phone.

She brought a plate of two biscuits and a slice of ham, along with the phone. After laying the phone near him, she picked up the pitcher of honey, liberally slathered the biscuits and then dove in.

Luke picked up his mug and sipped. He was being paranoid. Rocky hadn't answered his cell or his page. That made Luke nervous. Probably worrying for nothing. He checked his watch. He'd make another call in fifteen minutes.

"These biscuits are amazing." Sydney licked the honey from her fingers, and his thoughts headed straight for trouble. "I'd ask for the recipe if I knew how to cook."

Mama and Sydney both laughed.

Luke narrowed his gaze. "Why are you in such a good mood?"

Sydney widened her eyes on him. "Why wouldn't I be? We're safe and well-fed. And I had a terrific night's sleep."

He grunted. Glad someone had. He'd barely slept. Not because the couch was uncomfortable, but because his thoughts kept going back to Sydney—the curve of her hips, the firmness of her breasts, the soft mewing sounds she made when he suckled her.

Worse, her compassionate eyes and easy smile had made an imprint in his mind.

The physical longings he could deal with. She was attractive and sexy and what guy wouldn't want to get her in bed? It was the other feelings churning in his gut that bothered him. Feelings he'd never had for another client. He cared far more than he should.

Dangerous. Very dangerous.

For both of them.

"You want more ham?" Mama asked. "We have plenty. Biscuits and gravy, too."

He snapped out of his preoccupation. "No, thanks." He checked his watch again. "I'm going to go see what Jacques and Bernard are up to, and then make another phone call." He got up from the table and grabbed his plate. "You stick around here," he told Sydney.

She gave him a dry look. "No, I thought I'd go for a swim."

Honey glistened off her lower lip and he had to look away before he licked it off for her. "Keep your clothes packed," he said ignoring her sarcasm as he carried his plate and mug to the sink.

"They're packed."

Something oddly confident in her voice made him turn around.

She frowned. "Why? Is there something you haven't told me?"

Funny, he had the same thought. "No, but if we have to leave quickly I want to be ready."

"Luke." Mama's concerned voice drew his attention. "What happened with your friend?"

"I haven't been able to get a hold of him."

"That cannot be good," she said, her face creased with worry. "He knows you need information quickly, yes?"

He gave her a reassuring smile. "Too soon to fret. His cell phone could be out of range."

Sydney reached across the table for Mama's hand. "Really, don't worry. It's going to be all right."

Luke frowned. Sydney looked awfully damn confident. "I'm sure I'll reach him next time I call."

Mama nodded thoughtfully. "I think Jacques and Bernard are out back."

"Don't worry, Mama." Luke stopped to kiss her cheek and then went out the back door.

He saw Jacques sitting out by the storage shed, rifling through a burlap bag, but no sign of Bernard. Maybe he was passed out again. Luke hoped so. He had nothing against him. In fact, he felt sorry for him. The guy was close to Luke's age, but from hard living he looked more like fifty. But Luke didn't need any trouble.

He used the stairs and walked along the edge of the swamp toward Jacques, obsessively checking his watch again. What the hell? What difference did five minutes make? He stopped as he got close to Jacques and hit Redial.

He stared, confused at the number that came up on the screen. How did Willard's—

Son of a bitch.

Chapter Sixteen

"Toni will wash the dishes," Mama said firmly as soon as Sydney picked up the bottle of detergent. "That is her chore. You go tend to yourself."

Sydney hesitated, not wanting to seem useless, even though she couldn't remember the last time she'd washed dishes. That had probably been in college. Now, when she stayed at her apartment in the city, she ate out. When she stayed at the home she grew up in, Clara, their housekeeper, took care of everything, just as she had for the past twenty-seven years.

God, Sydney was spoiled. She hadn't really thought about it before. But most people did their own cooking and cleaning. Wiping off her bathroom vanity was the most effort she put into any housekeeping. Someone had always been there to pick up after her. Even now, she'd had to call Willard to help her out of this mess.

She left Mama in the kitchen wrapping up leftovers, grabbed a towel from her room and then headed for the bathhouse. She had no idea how long it would take Willard to get here. Toni's directions had been specific, if rather odd, requiring the use of landmarks. But Willard hadn't seemed bothered by them. He'd promised to come himself in the company plane, pick up her and Luke and then go back to Dallas in secret and decide what to do next.

As soon as she stepped outside, humid air clung to her skin like sap to a tree. It was tempting to go back inside and use the bathroom sink to wash up and then wait to get to Dallas for a long luxurious bath. But she knew she'd feel better getting on the plane with freshly washed hair.

"*Chérie*, there you are."

Sydney stopped at the sound of the familiar slimy heavily accented voice. She turned around just as Bernard stepped out from the shadow of the house. He grinned, silver gleaming from his lower teeth.

"Hi," she said, not wanting to be rude or start trouble. "If you're looking for Luke, he's down by the water."

He turned his head and spit on the ground. "What would I want from him?"

"Excuse me." She started to walk away, but he grabbed her arm. She yanked free and stumbled backward.

"Leave her alone."

Luke's voice came from behind, and then he pressed a hand to the small of her back until she regained her balance.

Bernard glared at him with hatred in his eyes. "*Quoi ça dit, bougre?*"

"You heard me." Luke moved between her and Bernard. "I think it's time you went home." He paused, a feral smile curving his mouth. "While you still have two legs to carry you."

Bernard had sobered up enough that he took a hard swing at Luke, who ducked in time and then grabbed the shorter man by the arm. He yanked it up behind his back, ignoring Bernard's angry cursing. He spewed French too fast and furious for Sydney to understand. Not that she couldn't guess at the gist of it.

Luke answered him in French and then released his arm. The man stumbled and fell to the ground. He used his shirt sleeve to wipe the back of his mouth where spit dripped from the corner, his angry resentment palpable.

"Get out of here." Luke stood over him, his fist clenched. "Now."

Bernard slowly, insolently got to his feet. He paused and stared with such venom on his face that Sydney shivered. Unhurriedly, he turned and swaggered down the gravel driveway and toward the woods.

"Thank you," Sydney said, sighing, deciding not to point out that she could have handled the situation.

Luke turned on her, his face furious. "What the hell did you do?"

She reared her head back. "Nothing. I was on my way to the bathhouse and he—"

"You called Willard, you stupid little fool."

She gasped. How did he— "Did Willard call you?"

"How long ago did you call?"

"While you were eating breakfast." She'd wanted to explain to him herself. Tell him she knew about Enrique and that she understood why trust was no longer easy for Luke.

He checked his watch and cursed viciously.

"It'll be all right, Luke." She laid a hand on his arm.

"He's coming personally to get us. No one else knows. He won't even tell the pilot where they're going or why."

Luke shook his head, his gaze drawn somewhere over her head, the pulse in his neck beating wildly. Finally, he looked at her again, anger and disappointment in his eyes. "Tell me exactly what he said."

"He's going to make a reservation at the Four Seasons hotel in Dallas under a fake name. We'll stay there until it's safe."

"What else?"

She shrugged. "That he's been frantic with worry."

Luke held her gaze, one eyebrow lifting slightly. "Did he call the police?"

She swallowed. Odd, he didn't mention anything about that. Of course, their conversation had been hurried. "He didn't say." She cleared her throat. "We didn't talk long."

He thought for a moment. "How would he know how to get here?"

"I gave him directions."

"How?"

"I asked Toni. She wrote them down for me."

He muttered a curse. "Did you mention Mama by name?" he asked in a dangerously quiet voice.

She nodded. "Toni said once you got past the landmarks, anyone could tell him where Mama lived, so I—" She broke off, her chest constricting at the look of disgust and fury on Luke's face. How could she make him understand? He didn't know Willard. Not really. Not the Willard she knew. How could he think she'd put Mama and the children in danger?

"Sydney, do you have any idea what you've done?"

"Look, I know about Enrique and what he did to you," she said, and he flinched. "I don't blame you for being distrustful. But Willard wouldn't—"

He cut her off. "I'm going to tell you something and I want you to listen good." He reached behind his back and pulled the gun out of the waistband of his jeans. "You're going to stay here and do everything Jacques tells you to do."

Her gaze stayed glued to the gun. "What are you going to do?"

"Did you hear me?"

"What are you going to do with that gun?"

"Sydney." He hooked a finger under her chin and forced her gaze up to his. "I hope I'm wrong about Willard. But I can't take any chances. Not with Mama and the kids. Do you understand?"

Her heart raced until she thought it would leap from her chest. "No, I don't understand why you need a gun."

"Don't be so friggin' naive." He jerked his hand away from her, and checked the gun's barrel. "Just stay here."

"Luke, please. Don't go. I'm begging you."

"You'll be safe here. Jacques' cousins live nearby. They all know how to use guns if need be."

"I'm not worried about me." Her voice broke. "I don't want you to get hurt."

"I thought you trusted Willard," he said with a mocking lift of his brow. "Why should I be in danger?"

She hesitated, hating his implication, hating that her own faith had been shaken.

"Look, we had great sex the other night but don't start reading too much into it. This is just a job for me. It's all about money, Sydney."

His words stung, and she flinched. "I don't believe you," she murmured.

He held her gaze for a moment and then his flickered away.

Jacques came up from the bank. He was still a ways away but she could see the concern on his face. "*Mon ami*, we have a problem?" he called to Luke.

"Yeah." Luke stuck the gun in the front part of his waistband. "I need to get to Joseph's Crossing. Is it faster to go by car or boat?"

"Boat." Jacques approached and looked from Luke to Sydney. "What is wrong?"

Luke quickly explained, while Jacques slid Sydney several sidelong glances. She tried to interrupt, hoping to find an ally in Jacques, but Luke stopped her and finished his conversation with Jacques in French. Most of which was spoken so quickly and with local inflection that she couldn't understand.

Finally, Luke looked at her. "I'll be back before dark. Stay put."

She clutched his arm. "Please, don't do this."

"I'm going to be waiting at the edge of the woods. If Willard comes alone, I'll bring him back here myself."

"So why do you need the gun?"

He exchanged a quick glance with Jacques and then pried her hand from his arm. "Take care of her, eh?"

Nodding, Jacques took a firm hold of her wrist. "*On va se revoir au ras de quatre heures.*"

Luke nodded back and then took off toward the swamp.

Knowing it was useless, Sydney said nothing. She also knew that they'd just agreed to meet at four o'clock. She didn't know where, but she sure as hell would be there, too.

LUKE FIGURED he had about three more hours before Willard could have gotten anywhere near Mama's house. Especially if the two thugs who'd shown up at the motel had taken the bait and were all the way to El Paso. Of course, Luke wasn't about to underestimate Willard's desperation. Who knew how many men he'd hired?

There was no way this should have happened. It was his fault for leaving the phone out where Sydney could get it. She'd been coddled all her life. She didn't get that even her most trusted friends would sell her out for money.

He flashed back on the hurt in her face when he'd told her he was only in it for the money. Better that she believed he had no feelings for her. Hell, he wasn't even sure what he felt. Didn't matter. Right now Sydney needed him, physically and emotionally. Once she got back to the safety of her own world, she'd forget him. Forget that incredible night they'd spent together.

But he couldn't think about her now. He had to focus. Make sure he got to Joseph's Crossing first.

He stopped rowing for a moment to flex his strained biceps. He'd left Mama's motorboat behind and used the canoe. It was slow but quiet, and he'd been rowing twice as hard to make up time.

He figured the two guys who killed the motel clerk would be the ones to show up. He had to get to the crossing in time and lead them away from Mama's house, get them lost deep in the swamps. Jacques knew where to meet him later.

Luke flexed one last time and then dipped the oars into the water. When he got through with those two, they'd beg him to call the police.

"YOU SHOULD NOT have let him go alone." Mama stood by the window, peering out over the swamp, wringing her hands and muttering prayers.

She'd repeated the same thing over two dozen times in the past two hours and even Sydney, who felt like hell over the trouble she'd caused, wished Mama would shut up.

"Enough, Sadie," Jacques said. "You know Luke. I had no choice. Anyway, that one, he is clever. He knows what he is doing."

"Call Pierre and Duke. Take them with you to look for him."

"And leave you alone with the children?" He made a sound of disgust and then checked his watch. When he raised his gaze, he sent a silent message to Mama.

Furtively, Sydney checked hers, too. Time dragged by. It was still a couple of hours before they were supposed to meet. She kept telling herself everything would be okay, that Luke would find out she was right to have called Willard. But a little voice deep inside wouldn't let her rest easy.

What if Willard told Rick and it turned out Rick was involved in the kidnapping? What if Willard's phone was tapped? Or what if he were followed? All kinds of scary possibilities occurred to her now that it was too late.

She was probably just being paranoid. Easy to do with the tension in the room thicker than fudge. But in the event she was wrong and Luke was in danger, she had to do something. She was the one they wanted. She had to find Luke or, better yet, their pursuers. Turn herself over to them. Once they had her, they'd leave Luke and Mama and the others alone. God, she hoped her sudden paranoia was for nothing. But if not, she couldn't allow Luke to die for her. She couldn't even bear the thought.

The kids had been sent to stay with Mama's cousin in town. With Mama glued to the window and Jacques busy trying to calm her, Sydney casually headed toward the hall.

"Where are you going?" Jacques asked before she'd taken three steps.

"To my room," Sydney said airily, "to pack. My godfather should be arriving soon and I'll be heading to Dallas."

Jacques gave her a pitying look and then indicated with his chin that she could continue.

As soon as she got in the room, she closed the door and went straight to the window. It opened easily and quietly, and she climbed out without incident. She had only one way she could run without being seen, and she took off in that direction, the same way Bernard had gone earlier.

Luke said Jacques had cousins who lived near by. Hopefully, they were better specimens than Bernard. God knew, he wasn't her first choice for a guide, and she hoped there'd be someone else whose help she could enlist. But if Bernard was her only option to get to Luke, well, there was no choice.

Fortunately, the path led away from the water and was well traveled enough that she didn't fear getting lost. Not much, anyway. The strange croaking and chirping noises unnerved her and every little movement on the ground had her jumping. But it wasn't long before the trees started to ebb and she could see a building in the clearing.

It was a house not nearly as large or as well maintained as Mama's; in fact, it wasn't more than a shack. But she hurried toward it, praying there'd be someone she could convince or bribe to help her.

She got to the door but before she could knock, Bernard sauntered toward her from around the corner of the house. His swarthy face creased in a grin.

"You are looking for me, *chérie*?" He seemed sober, which was encouraging, but she still didn't like him.

"Do you live here?"

"*Oui*." He moved closer and she forced herself to stay where she was.

"Anyone else?"

"My brother and nephew." He took out a slim brown cigarette, lit it and placed it between his lips. "Why?"

"Are they here?"

He shook his head. "In town."

She took a breath, reminded herself to stay calm, professional. Treat this like a business deal back at the office. "I need someone to help me get to Joseph's Crossing."

He frowned, his gaze briefly roaming the front of her shirt. "Why?"

"To meet someone."

"Who?"

"That doesn't matter," she said, knowing that the bad blood between him and Luke could get in the way. "Are you interested?"

"How much?"

"Five hundred dollars."

He opened his mouth and the cigarette fell to the ground. "You crazy?"

"We'd have to leave right away."

His gaze again ran down the front of her body. "You have the money?"

"Not on me. You'll get paid after."

He studied her for a moment and then he smiled, the silver gleaming from his mouth. "Let's go."

She started to follow and then realized Bernard was headed toward the water. "Wait. I thought Joseph's Crossing was on land."

"*Oui*, but it is easier and faster by water."

Her chest tightened. "How much faster?"

"Very much faster," he said and pointed to an old motorboat tied to an unstable-looking wooden dock. "By land, it could take hours. By motor boat, half the time."

Sydney stared at the murky water, the lump growing in her throat threatening to block her air passage. She couldn't do it. She didn't care how many people traveled the swamp without harm. She just couldn't...

"Come on," Bernard said as he jumped onto the boat. "Your friend is waiting."

Luke.

Oh, God. She had to get to him before anyone else did.

She prayed she wouldn't faint and tried not to close her eyes as she accepted Bernard's help to get on board. Immediately, she sat on the roughly crafted bench seat.

Bernard started the engine, pulled out a small bottle of liquor from inside his shirt and gave her a grin that made her shiver.

Chapter Seventeen

Luke paddled more slowly as the canoe sliced silently through the gentle waves of the swamp, leaving little wake other than a slight parting of the green scum. Mist still clung to the water, sinuously winding through the mangroves and cypress knees, lending a mystic aura to the bayous of his childhood.

The hardness of the Glock pressed into his belly. He remembered when they'd returned it to him after his year in prison. The shallow smiles, the pats on the back. He spat into the scum-covered water and something rose to snap at the spit, whatever it was unafraid of the paddle and the long shape of the canoe. Luke heard a splash from the nearby shore as a small alligator slid into the water to see what might be competing for his food.

The morning sun barely penetrated this deeply into the swamp, and Luke found himself unaccountably nervous each time his path took him through a patch of sunlight—few of the swamp creatures, with the exception of the hardy little deer and the gators—had much use for sunlight, and on this mission, neither did Luke.

Although he'd been paddling hard for Joseph's Crossing, as he neared the spit of land where the narrow road curved out close to the lightning-struck tree, he suddenly noticed the absence of spring peepers—the little frogs whose near constant presence in the swamp became subliminal—he only noticed them when they stilled. All along, they'd quieted briefly at his passing, but as he approached the area where the road neared the marshes, they were already quiet. Luke expertly guided the canoe next to a fallen tree and let the prow carve a deep gouge in the mud of the shore.

He stepped out and pulled the canoe a few feet farther and then crept forward, peering around the heavy growths of Spanish moss to see the road. He heard the tiny frogs in his wake resume their chorus, emphasizing once again the fact that only on this bit of soggy earth was there a disturbance of the natural order.

He saw the car before he saw the men; a black two-door Lincoln sedan, dramatically out of place in this land of pickups and rolling antiques.

He pulled his gun from his waistband and clicked the safety off. Then he slipped quietly sideways and crouched, scouting for the still-invisible men. He paused, then moved toward the muted murmur of voices.

"…said something about a tree that had been hit by lightning."

"So why are you wasting time looking at that damned map? Hell, this road isn't even on it. Let's just find this Mama—whoever—and get this over with."

Beneath the moss as below a heavy theater curtain, Luke saw two pairs of legs, in fashionable cargo pants as out of place as their car. As he heard the men's words, a chill went through him and bile rose in his throat. He raised his pistol and fired twice.

The two ran behind their car as they reached into matching windbreakers to pull their own weapons. The hiss from the left front tire of the car filled the air. Luke grabbed a young pine and shook it, and the two men fired wildly at the commotion.

"Come and get it, *mon ami*," Luke yelled. He shook the sapling again, then ran down the narrow spit of land for the water, making as much noise as he could.

He hit the shallow bayou at a dead run, splashing heavily for a small island a hundred feet away. Just short of the shore, he heard the nearly simultaneous crack of a pistol behind him and the heavy thunk of a bullet hitting a tree in front of him, wood chips flying. He ran into the trees and crouched, peering back across the water.

The two figures, nearly twins in their matching pants and windbreakers, stood arguing.

"Snakes, man. I'm scared of snakes."

"Don't worry. If you're making noise, they won't get you. That's Luke Boudreau, man. We gotta get him."

The Texas accents carried farther in the bayous than the men could have known, and Luke smiled grimly as he heard. If he could lure them far enough, he and Jacques could make them talk, and then Sydney would know who her friends were. Her real friends. He took a deep breath.

Once again, he ran for the water, exposing himself briefly, staying in the shallows. Another shot rang out, then another. The sound of ricochets came too close to his pumping legs. Damn! He was more out of shape than he thought.

He hit another soggy patch of land surrounded by water and ducked behind a tree, listening.

Sure enough, the two Texas gunmen were splashing after him. Timing was everything now.

He stuck the pistol securely in his waistband and looked about, keeping one ear open for the approach of the two gunmen. Although Luke had spent years in the swamps, the details changed year in and year out with every rainfall. What he needed to do was keep track of the main features so he didn't get lost himself. And keep the men from finding their way back to the road.

The combination of splashing feet and heavy breathing came closer, and Luke ran again, heading for another small island. He made no effort at silence.

Sheltered by the thick vegetation, he again assessed the options ahead of him. To the left was a marshy area, several hundred acres of high reeds and shallow water, but relatively light and open. To the right lay more mangroves and Spanish moss, a tangled skein of small islands, quicksand and primordial ferns. And, if one went far enough that way, dry land.

A bullfrog chose that moment to issue a querying mating call, and one of the Texans fired two shots toward the sound. The shots echoed through the swamp, and now there were no spring peepers calling.

Grinning, Luke edged toward the reeds, waiting for the men to get closer. For him, the marsh would be something of a rest. The men could track him easily by following the weaving and broken reeds, but would be unable to get a clear shot. If he could get them just a few hundred yards farther, he could lead them into the deep swamp again, then get back to the mainland himself and enlist Jacques to help corral the two.

Of course, he had to get across a couple of hundred feet of open water before he hit the marsh. Preferably without getting shot.

Luke took a deep breath and charged forward.

He was halfway to cover when doubt struck him. Although the water didn't even reach his knees, he felt like he had lead weights around his ankles. He was exposed, the sunlight making him an easy target, and the area between his shoulder blades itched as if waiting for the bullet that would end it all. His lungs burned with effort. Gunshots rang out behind him.

Then Mama's face seemed to swim in the air before him. "You can do whatever you need to, *mon cher*," she said. "And my dreams do not lie." She smiled at him, and suddenly Luke found himself in the safety of the reeds.

He turned and fired a shot wildly to his rear, solely to slow his pursuers and then went a few feet farther before pausing to catch his breath. Oddly, both his heart and his feet felt lighter, and it was with renewed vigor that he strode forward. These men would never get close to Mama. Or Sydney.

His pursuers were clumsier than he'd thought, and Luke had time to pause at the far side of the marsh. If he remembered correctly, there was an abandoned Cajun fishing shack not far away, and if he could get to it, he might be able to arrange an ambush of some kind. Since the two gunmen were still scrambling through the reeds, inexpertly following his trail, he set off into deep swamp at barely a walk.

Entering the shadows again, Luke stayed as much as

possible on the small islands, breaking ferns and small trees so the men would be able to follow. He almost felt sorry for them. This had been his game from the start, and these two obviously had little of the necessary skills to survive in the bayou. As he heard them break out of the reeds he fired another shot so they'd know the way, and continued methodically marking his trail.

Whenever the men neared, Luke would hurry ahead. As he rounded a huge group of mangroves, he came upon a small cove. On the other side, a short dock lay half in the water, and just beyond, a ramshackle building, overgrown with vines, and surrounded by cedars and ferns.

He skirted the water as much as possible, approaching the shack cautiously with his gun at the ready. Although it looked abandoned, any number of creatures, some of them human, might have taken refuge there.

Luke picked his way through the overgrown bushes, stepped over a fallen tree and neared the door. He brushed away a giant spider web and pushed aside the remains of a crude plank door to step into the one-room shack.

The remains of an ancient moldy mattress sagged on a rusted iron frame, and there was a wood-burning stove in the corner, also rusting. A hole in the ceiling above showed where the tumbled stovepipe had been. Everywhere lay the evidence of human and animal habitation. Luke picked up a broken rake handle and poked at a pile of rubble, then jumped back as a large swamp rat scrambled for the door.

Using the piece of wood as a tool, Luke quickly searched the cabin, looking for anything that might be useful. As he brushed at one pile of trash, he struck something metal. He moved away the stuff on top and found himself looking at an old bear trap. He carefully moved it and pried at the jaws until it was fully open, then poked the rusted piece in the middle until the aged springs snapped the trap together. Grinning, he picked the trap up by its chain and headed out the door, continuing past the cabin.

As he entered the woods, he fired another shot to keep the gunmen heading in the right direction and was startled to hear a gasp from somewhere in front of him. He set the trap down carefully and edged forward. As he pushed his way past the ferns and moss, he saw a flash of white. The figure moved. "Sydney," he whispered. Then, louder, "Sydney."

She turned to him fearfully, then her eyes widened in recognition and she stumbled to him. "Luke. Oh God, Luke."

She fell into his arms and he held her for a few seconds. "What the hell happened to you? What are you doing out here? Jacques..."

"Bernard promised to take me to you, but once we were into the swamp..."

Luke pushed her out to arm's length and looked coldly at her torn blouse and tear-streaked face. "That son of a bitch. I'll tear his heart out."

Several large splashes and a snapping twig brought Luke back to awareness. "You've got to get out of here." Swiftly, he racked his brain, trying to remember the easiest path to the road. He pointed through the trees. "Go that way for about a hundred yards. You'll—"

She vigorously shook her head. "I heard the shots. Was it—"

"Not Willard."

"Who?"

"The guys from the motel. You have to go, Sydney. Now."

"No, it's me they want. Let me go to them. Let me—" She tried to pull away, but he held on to her arm.

"Dammit, Sydney. You're going to get us both killed. Is that what you want?"

"No." Her teary eyes flashed with anger. "I don't want anything to happen to you, Luke. I couldn't bear it."

"Then listen to me." He glanced around and then pointed. "Go that way until you come to a path. Follow it to the right until you come to the road. Go right until you see a black car with a flat tire. Go out that point and you'll find a canoe pulled up next to a dead tree."

"Luke. I can't take a canoe." She shook her head, eyes wide with fear.

He grabbed her roughly by the shoulders, mindful of the sound of the two Texans going through the cabin. "It's the only way. If I can't stop these two…"

"But a canoe…"

"Stay close to the shore on your left until you come to Joseph's Crossing. Stay there until I come for you."

"But Luke…"

He could hear the men's voices again, and he pushed her, hard, toward the path. "Go. Now. For God's sake, Sydney."

She stumbled, regained her footing, then kissed him and whispered, "I love you," before she turned and fled in the direction he'd indicated.

Luke was stunned, but caught himself quickly and ran in the opposite direction. He picked up the trap and then took off again, breaking branches as loudly as he could. When he reached water, he jumped in, splashing more than necessary, making all the noise he could. He smiled grimly as he heard his pursuers following.

He splashed through the water to the next fern-and cedar-covered island, quickly breaking a few small tupelos to mark his way. Then he dug into the mud with his hands and laid the bear trap into the hole. He broke some ferns and laid them over the trap. He stepped back and looked at the setup, nodding to himself in approval, then ran ahead to duck behind a large cedar. He crouched, leaning with his back against the rough bark, holding his weapon at the ready. He waited.

In the distance, the spring peepers were singing again. A distant alligator roared once and bullfrogs joined the chorus. A crane screeched. His pursuers reached the shore and paused, whispering to each other.

Luke found himself holding his breath. What was going on? They couldn't have seen his trap—they weren't close enough. A branch cracked to his right and he turned awkwardly on his haunches, weapon pointed toward the sound. Something man-sized and careless pushed its way noisily through the underbrush.

Suddenly Bernard stumbled into view, scratched and bloodied by branches. He stopped at the water's edge, swaying, probably drunk, peering about as if to get his bearings.

Despite his earlier statement, Luke was stunned when a volley of shots boomed out across the swamp and Bernard practically flew backward to fall across a small dead pine.

"Was that him?" It was one of the Texans.

Luke couldn't hear the other man's response, but did hear the men as they moved toward him again. "Damned Cajuns," one of them said.

There was a loud snap and an inhuman scream. Luke stepped out from behind the cedar, firing back along his path as he moved—four, five, six shots.

For a moment, he thought he'd missed. The tall man stood stock still, weapon dangling from his fingers, a look of surprise on his face. Then he crumpled to the ground and another scream came from his partner, lying at his feet, caught in the trap.

Luke edged forward until he stood over the two men.

"God, the pain," the live man groaned. "Please, get this guy off me."

Luke uncocked his gun, clicked on the safety and shoved the weapon into his waistband. "Yeah, I'll get him off you." He bent to the task. "But you're going to be answering some questions."

Chapter Eighteen

She'd said she loved him. She didn't mean it, of course. Trauma did strange things to people's heads. Messed with their minds.

Luke looked over at Sydney, sitting only inches away from him in the cab, her leg brushing his, her gaze focused out the window, her mind miles away.

The plane ride back to Dallas had been quiet and somber. He would have preferred to drive, give Sydney time to digest all that had happened, but they had to return quickly and confront Willard before he discovered his henchman had failed.

Ernie, the coward who'd lived, gave up Willard without a second's hesitation. Luke would never forget the look of shocked disbelief on Sydney's face. She'd physically recoiled, the hurt and pain shadowing her eyes almost more than Luke could bear.

Never in his life had he wanted to protect someone, cradle her in his arms and make all the hurt go away. God, she didn't deserve this. Not Sydney.

"It's not too late to call the police," he said quietly, drawing her attention.

She shook her head and reached over to take Luke's hand.

"He could have a gun."

"You don't have to go in with me. In fact, I'd prefer you didn't."

"Not gonna happen." He squeezed her hand. He knew she wanted to protect him. She was really something. Conquering her fear and braving the swamp to get to him.

Being ready to confront Willard.

That idea Luke wasn't crazy about. But she'd insisted. She wanted to give Willard a chance to explain. She wanted him to look her in the eyes and tell her why.

Luke could do that. Greed. He'd bet everything he owned that it all boiled down to money. Because Sydney was worth one hell of a lot of it.

Which was one of the reasons a relationship between them wouldn't work. She was a "have" and he was a "have-not." The past few days, she'd had to depend on him for survival, and that slanted the dynamics of the relationship. When she felt less vulnerable, her feelings toward him would change. Resentment might even build.

He'd turned her world upside down. It wouldn't matter that Willard set the ugly chain of events in motion. She wouldn't want to focus on the betrayal. Easier to dwell on the terror of the past four days, and blame Luke for the motel clerk's death and her encounter with Bernard.

The cab pulled up in front of the stately Wainwright building, and Luke paid the driver. He'd figured Sydney would be reluctant to get out of the car, but he had to jump out to keep up with her.

He caught her at the revolving door and pulled her

aside as soon as they entered the lobby. "I don't like this, Sydney. It's dangerous and stupid."

She gave him a sad smile. "Probably. But I have to do it this way."

Luke ran a hand down his face. At six-twenty, the lobby was mostly deserted. A few people were still around, but were too busy talking or heading for the elevators to the parking garage to notice them.

Still, he didn't want to take any chance that Willard could be warned that they were in the building. He took her arm and hurried her to the elevators.

"There's a private one to the top over there," she said, but he shook his head.

"No, it stops too close to Willard's office. No sense broadcasting our arrival."

She nodded, seeming amazingly calm.

Shit, she was probably still in shock. Didn't know what she was doing. It had only been a matter of hours since she'd learned that Willard had hired those two men to kill both him and her. Maybe he ought to flat out tell her she couldn't do this. Force her to stay in a hotel until the police had the bastard in custody.

The elevator doors opened, and she calmly stepped inside and pressed the button to take them to the Wainwright suite of offices as if she'd merely been returning from lunch instead of five days in hell.

Luke furtively stuck his hand behind his back to feel his Glock tucked in his jeans. He didn't want to mention the gun and frighten her, but no way would he face Willard without it. As far as Sydney knew, Willard didn't own a gun, but obviously there was a lot she didn't know about the man.

When they got to the top floor and the elevator doors opened, Sydney hesitated. So did Luke, hoping she'd reconsidered. But she lifted a shaking hand to push the hair off her face, cleared her throat and took a step.

Abruptly, he laid a hand on her arm and then preceded her out of the car to the reception area. The place was deserted. Eerily quiet. The lights were still on, but the individual office doors were closed.

"Is this normal?" he whispered, keeping his gaze trained on the empty hall.

She shook her head. "At least a few people are still working."

"Willard's office still down at the end of the hall?"

"Yes." Her voice came out barely a whisper.

"It's not too late to change your mind."

She visibly swallowed. "Let's go."

He put a restraining hand on her arm. "Stay behind me."

"But—"

He didn't give her a chance to argue, but took the lead, making sure she stayed directly behind him as he started down the hall toward Willard's office. In the elevator, he'd transferred his gun so that it was quickly accessible. For her sake, he hoped he didn't have to use it.

Willard's office door was open, but so were two others and Luke turned to give her a questioning frown. She pointed and mouthed one was hers, the other Rick's. He nodded and put a finger to his lips to remind her to stay silent.

Just as he got to Willard's door, he heard a noise inside. Luke grabbed his gun and raised it before crossing the threshold.

Sydney gasped.

Sitting behind the desk, Rick looked up from a piece of paper he'd been reading, his expression dazed. He saw Sydney. Shock widened his eyes and he jumped to his feet, letting the paper float to the desk.

"Sydney!" He came around the desk and wrapped his arms around her. "Thank God."

She whimpered a little, burying her face between his neck and shoulder, and then pulled back and sniffed. "Where's Willard?"

Rick frowned, his gaze going to Luke.

"It's important, Rick," Sydney said, forcing his attention back to her. "I'll explain everything later."

"He left." He sent Luke another wary glance, and then went back to the desk and retrieved the paper and an envelope. "He gave me this letter, and told me to give you this." He handed the envelope to Sydney. "He looked as if he'd been run over by a train. What the hell is going on?"

"How long ago did he leave?" Luke asked, checking his watch at the same time.

"About half an hour."

"We have time to stop him. He's probably headed for the airport but—"

"No." Sydney had opened the envelope and was reading something scribbled in longhand. She looked up. "Let him go."

"No way."

"I mean it, Luke." Her eyes pleaded, but her voice was firm. "Let him go."

Luke shook his head. "You're not thinking straight, Sydney."

"Yes, I am," she said calmly and went back to the letter.

"Will somebody please tell me what the hell is going on." Rick looked from his sister to Luke. He hadn't shaved in a couple of days and the skin below his eyes puffed from sleeplessness.

Luke made a motion with his head for him to step aside while Sydney read the letter. The poor guy obviously had been worried and deserved an explanation.

During the entire time he filled Rick in, Luke kept his gaze on Sydney's pale face as she read the letter for a second time. She blinked a few times, he suspected to hold back the tears, and then finally looked up. She said nothing, but handed him the letter.

Rick came out of his stunned silence to mutter expletives of disbelief while reading over Luke's shoulder.

Willard admitted everything. How he'd taken aggressive stock market risks that had ruined him financially. He'd borrowed company money that he'd intended on repaying. But he couldn't do it before Sydney sold the company, when all accounting would be dissected and made public.

He'd only wanted to scare her off and buy some time, but he panicked. He asked for her forgiveness. Not a mention of how he'd planned to frame Luke. Not that it mattered.

"This is incredible." Rick looked up, his face in total disbelief. "You can't let him get away with this, Syd."

She sank in one of the chairs. "You think he's gotten away? Can you even begin to imagine what kind of hell he'll live in for the rest of his life?"

"Not hellish enough." Rick cursed viciously. "He needs to be locked up. He was worried about the embezzlement going public. Let his ass get dragged through a trial, his face plastered across the front page of the newspaper."

Sydney smiled through the pain and disappointment shadowing her face. God, Luke would give anything to erase her hurt. But he knew only time would do that.

"Rick, do me a favor. Leave Luke and I alone for a moment."

Obviously, Rick's anger hadn't subsided and she quickly added, "And no phone calls to the police. I mean it."

He glanced at Luke. "I don't agree, but I'll back off."

"Thank you." She smiled, looking tired. Totally drained.

"I do have some calls to make, though. Margaret has been worried sick. So have Jeff and Julie."

A brief frown furrowed her brows. "Is Margaret the only one in the office who knew I was missing?"

"Yes. We thought it best."

Luke had expected more of a reaction at the mention of Jeff, but only a trace of curiosity laced her voice when she asked, "How do Jeff and Julie know each other?"

Rick shrugged. "I think they just met the other night. Jeff had just come by when Willard claimed to have gotten the ransom call, and he asked Jeff to discreetly find out what he could at the salon."

Sydney looked at Luke. "Why would he do that?"

"So Julie or the receptionist would confirm that you were picked up by someone in a black Town Car. You'd been getting threatening letters. Short leap to believe you'd been kidnapped. After we were both dead, his men would make it look like I killed you and they shot me while trying to save you."

Sydney gazed out the window at the Dallas skyline, and muttered, "Jeff couldn't find me so he screwed Julie."

Rick snorted. "What?"

She brought her attention back to them with a wry smile. "Never mind." She sighed and laid her head back against the leather chair and closed her eyes.

"Okay, I'll leave you guys alone." Rick gave Luke a curious look before he left the office and closed the door.

Sydney opened her eyes and smiled wanly. "What a day, huh?"

"That might be the biggest understatement of the year."

Luke walked to the credenza behind the desk and helped himself to water from a crystal carafe. He poured a glass for each of them.

He'd hang around for a while and make sure she was okay. She was still in shock, whether she knew it or not. As it wore off and she got stronger, she wouldn't need him, and he'd head back to Los Angeles. Make plans to fly to Brazil. Find Enrique. Show him what it felt like to have your entire life ruined.

Assuming she paid him the fee Willard had promised. Which Luke felt certain she would.

Willard.

Luke still couldn't believe she was willing to let the bastard go free. She had the right and resources to make him pay. Of course, Willard wouldn't get away—there were four dead bodies for which he was responsible. The authorities wouldn't be as forgiving as Sydney.

"When do you think they'll have Bernard's funeral?" she asked, as she accepted the water.

"Why?"

"I think we should go." She blinked. "I mean, I'll definitely go, but I'd like it if you go with me."

Luke stared at her in disbelief. "He tried to attack you."

"I'm not going for him, but for his family." Her eyes saddened. "He died because of me. Oh, and I want to do something for the family. You know, financially speaking. I'm sure you can help me decide how to go about doing that."

"You're amazing."

Her brows drew together. "I don't understand."

He shook his head. "I still think you should go after Willard."

Hurt washed over her face and he was sorry he'd mentioned the name. She sighed. "Even if I'd found out about the money, I wouldn't have cared. Of course, I would have been horribly disappointed, but I would have given anything he needed to cover his debts. I don't doubt he loved me. He made a huge mistake that he'll pay for the rest of his life."

"A mistake?" Luke laughed humorlessly and shook his head.

"A by-product of being human, as my mother would say." She smiled. "I wish you could have met her. You would've loved her. And she would have—what's wrong?"

Luke rubbed his tired eyes. "I don't get it. You were so awesome, keeping it together with the helicopter breathing down our necks, braving the swamp, the whole thing. And now you want to be a doormat. For God's sake, the guy tried to have you killed."

Sydney's lips curved in a patient smile that annoyed him. "So I should let him finish me off?"

"You're not making sense."

"Revenge is draining and nonproductive, Luke. Why should I give him the power to ruin my life? I want to move forward and be happy." She looked beseechingly at him. "I hope my future includes you."

Luke turned away to stare out the window. The city looked different from up here. Quiet and peaceful. This was Sydney's world, far removed from the strains of everyday life. She could buy isolation and bury her head in the sand if she wanted, wait for the unpleasantness to pass.

There was so much she didn't understand about the real world. Where he lived. Where hard-earned respect could be squashed with one lie. Where so-called friends turned their backs while your entire life went up in flames.

Sure, she'd suffered a hard blow with Willard's betrayal, and he didn't think she suffered any less because she was rich, but she at least she had options, resources to help her forget.

"Luke?"

Reluctantly, he turned back to her.

"Please, don't shut me out."

He couldn't meet her pleading eyes. "You don't understand, Sydney."

"Then explain. Help me to understand."

He exhaled sharply when she laid a hand on his arm. Not a good thing. Her slightest touch made him weak. Made him forget how different they were. Made him want to believe something could develop between them.

Not wanting to come right out and shake her off, he moved his arm to shove the unruly hair back from his face, effectively breaking contact. "Look," he said gently, moving away from her. "After you've taken care of business here, go on a cruise or to one of those spas and pamper yourself for a few weeks."

Angry color rose in her cheeks. "If I thought you were serious, I'd be highly insulted."

Wrong thing to say, he realized, but he was serious. "Sydney, you're still in shock." Probably in denial, too. And this was just the tip of the iceberg. "You'll need to take it easy. I have business to take care of myself, so—"

"Enrique?"

Luke turned back to stare out the window again. How well she already knew him. Didn't mean he'd let her interfere. The score he had to settle was between him and Enrique.

"What will you do when you find him?" she asked softly.

"I don't know." Luke hesitated. All he'd ever thought about was finding the bastard. He'd dreamt about squeezing his hands around his neck and listening to him beg. "Bring him back here to stand trial. Let him get dragged through the mud like I did."

"Will that help?"

"This is none of your damn business, Sydney," he said, his ominous tone a warning she didn't heed.

She maneuvered herself between him and the window and got right in his face. "Of course it is. I love you. I want you to be able to love me back. But it won't work with bitterness and hate in the way."

He stared at her hard. "You don't love me. You've needed me. Had to depend on me. That created a certain bond. You have a therapist? Go ask her about it. It's textbook stuff."

"I know. I considered that possibility." She shook her head, her gaze even with his, so full of conviction he wanted to believe her. "But that's not the case. I do love you."

"Sydney…look at me. I come from the swamps." He gestured around the richly appointed office, the furnishings alone worth more than all his possessions. "This is your world."

The hurt in her eyes made his gut clench. Then her gaze narrowed and she took a step closer. "You're letting money come between us?"

"No." He had to stop and think for a moment. "We come from different places."

"So, you come from the swamps. Is that who you are?" she asked, her voice low and steady. When he didn't respond, she added, "Is that how you define yourself?"

"I hadn't really thought about it." The disappointment in her face got to him and he retracted. "I guess not."

"Good, because this isn't who I am either. You're the one who places so much importance on money." He started to object but she held up a hand. "What did you think, a cruise or health spa would help me get over you? If you think money buys happiness, think again. It turned Enrique against you, and Willard against me."

"Maybe it will destroy us, too," he murmured, wishing she weren't so damn close. Her honeyed scent alone drove him crazy. Made him want to believe all her rationalizations.

"For us, pride is a bigger stumbling block," she said softly, the pleading in her eyes his final undoing.

He grabbed her upper arms, holding her in place. Afraid she'd kiss him. More afraid he'd kiss her back. "What do you want from me, Sydney?"

"Do you love me?" She didn't blink. Just stared up at him with total trust.

Jeez, he couldn't even lie. "Yes."

She smiled. "That's all I want."

His throat tightened. "Do you know what you're asking?"

"I haven't asked for anything," she said, remaining perfectly still, not making a single move to touch him. "I'm hoping you'll follow your heart."

He stared at her a moment, emotion threatening his composure. She was amazing. Smart, beautiful, rich. And she wanted him.

If only he didn't have so damn much baggage…

Screw Enrique.

The thought came from nowhere. Like an epiphany, and Luke knew he couldn't give the bastard another ounce of power. He'd already stolen so much of his life and his happiness. He wouldn't let Enrique rob him of Sydney, too.

Luke let go of one of her arms and lifted his hand to touch her soft hair. "So you think we have a chance, huh?"

The relief that lit her eyes humbled him. "More than a chance. A whole lifetime together."

"I love you, Sydney." He slid his arms around her and pulled her against him before she saw the glassiness in his eyes.

Epilogue

The next Thanksgiving

"Look at that bird. So nice and plump and golden." Sighing, Mama clasped her hands to her bosom and stepped back so Luke could close the oven door.

Toni groaned. "Isn't dinner ready yet? I'm starving."

"Half an hour longer. Go set the table." Mama made a shooing motion, and Toni, Diego and two younger boys who'd joined Mama's flock since Luke and Sydney's last visit, filed out of the kitchen with long faces.

Jacques chuckled. "That is some big oven you bought her. It came last week and already all the neighbors know she can bake bread and roast meat at the same time."

"Not all the neighbors." Mama lifted her chin and grabbed a dish towel. "I haven't talked to Madeleine for two weeks."

Luke and Sydney laughed, and Sydney couldn't help giving her new husband a smug smile. He'd sworn up and down Mama would hate a modern commercial range. Sydney had known otherwise. Even she was learning to cook a little, Cajun dishes mostly, and she sure as heck appreciated modern kitchen conveniences.

"I'm hungry, too," Luke said, glancing at his watch. "Too much longer and we'll have to take dinner to go."

Sydney elbowed him in the ribs. She felt bad enough cutting their time short here, but they had Julie and Jeff's wedding to attend tomorrow. In fact, Sydney was Julie's matron of honor.

Mama's resigned sigh didn't help. "What about Christmas? Will you come here?"

"Mama," Luke said, "I'm sure Sydney has her own traditions."

Sydney hesitated. She had promised Julie they'd all spend Christmas and New Year's together. Their renewed friendship was still so fragile. Although Julie had been innocent of Willard's plot, she still felt guilty over sleeping with Jeff the night he'd gone to the salon tracking Sydney's steps.

She didn't even hold it against Jeff. It had been fate, Sydney decided. Julie was deliriously happy, and Sydney was...

He and Rick had worked hard together to divest the company. When they were done, even the union was happy. The small section the three of them had decided to keep intact more than provided them with a challenge.

Sydney brightened. "Why don't you all come to Dallas? We'll send the company plane for you. It would be an easy trip."

"Mama, please, Mama, please." Toni came flying out of the other room, her palms pressed together in prayer. "I want to fly in a plane. I want to go to Dallas. Please."

Mama frowned. "I don't know." She looked at Jacques, who gave his trademark shrug. "I'll have to think on it."

Luke slid his arm around her shoulders. "Now, Mama, you wouldn't want to miss out on the surprise we have for you."

Sydney pressed her lips together to keep from grinning like an idiot and giving herself away. But her hand automatically went to her still-flat stomach. She caught Luke's wink and sighed to herself. She couldn't have planned a better ever-after herself.

Like a phantom in the night
comes an exciting promotion from

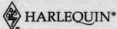
HARLEQUIN®

INTRIGUE®

ECLIPSE

GOTHIC ROMANCE

Look for a provocative
gothic-themed thriller each month
by your favorite Intrigue authors!
Once you surrender to the classic
blend of chilling suspense and
electrifying romance in these
gripping page-turners, there will
be no turning back....

Available wherever Harlequin books are sold.

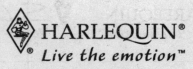

HARLEQUIN®
Live the emotion™

www.eHarlequin.com

HIE3

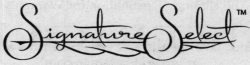

SPOTLIGHT

**Every month we'll spotlight
original stories from Harlequin
and Silhouette Books' Shining Stars!**

Fantastic authors, including:

- Debra Webb
- Julie Elizabeth Leto
- Merline Lovelace
- Rhonda Nelson

**Plus, value-added Bonus Features
are coming soon to a book near you!**

- Author Interviews
- Bonus Reads
- The Writing Life
- Character Profiles

SIGNATURE SELECT SPOTLIGHT
On sale January 2005

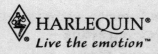

If you enjoyed what you just read,
then we've got an offer you can't resist!

Take 2 bestselling
love stories FREE!

Plus get a FREE surprise gift!

Enter the compelling and unpredictable world of Silhouette Bombshell

We're pulling out the stops to bring you four high-octane reads per month featuring women of action who always save the day and get— or get away from—their men. Guaranteed.

Available at your local retailer in January 2005:

STELLA, GET YOUR MAN
by Nancy Bartholomew

DECEIVED
by Carla Cassidy

ALWAYS LOOK TWICE
by Sheri WhiteFeather

THE HUNTRESS
by Crystal Green

Sexy. Savvy. Suspenseful.

Silhouette®

BOMBSHELL™

More Than Meets the Eye

SPOTLIGHT

Dying To Play

Debra Webb

When FBI agent Trace Callahan arrives in Atlanta to investigate a baffling series of multiple homicides, deputy chief of detectives Elaine Jentzen isn't prepared for the immediate attraction between them. And as they hunt to find the killer known as the Gamekeeper, it seems that Trace is singled out as his next victim...unless Elaine can stop the Gamekeeper before it's too late.

Available January 2005.

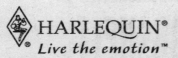

Live the emotion™

Exclusive Bonus Features:
Author Interview
Sneak Preview...
and more!